NOWHERE TO RUN

The wolverine slunk nearer. Its rounded ears, its powerful body, its thick legs, its wide paws with their curved claws, its glistening fangs—the predator was a living portrait of ferocity.

Shakespeare had the Hawken pointed at the ground. He slowly started to level it but stopped when the wolverine snarled and coiled. Freezing, Shakespeare braced himself, but the glutton did not spring. For the moment it was content to study him as he was studying it.

"You don't quite know what to make of me, do you?" Shakespeare began inching backward. "I must be ugly by your standards, but you're no beauty by mine."

The wolverine let out a strange cry, half-growl, half-hiss.

Shakespeare's amazement turned to shock when he heard an answering cry. Not from far away. From directly behind him.

Shakespeare half turned.

A second wolverine was crouched eight feet away. The first one had kept him occupied while its sibling snuck up unnoticed. Now they had him boxed in on the bluff's brink…

The *Wilderness* series:

#49
WILDERNESS

WOLVERINE

David Thompson

LEISURE BOOKS NEW YORK CITY

Dedicated to Judy, Joshua and Shane.

A LEISURE BOOK®

August 2006

Published by

Dorchester Publishing Co., Inc.
200 Madison Avenue
New York, NY 10016

ISBN 0-8439-5711-5

Printed in the United States of America.

Visit us on the web at www.dorchesterpub.com.

WOLVERINE

PROLOGUE

The female's nose twitched. From out of the valley wafted scents new to her. Tantalizing scents that made her halt and lift her head up into the wind.

Behind her, her five offspring also stopped and sniffed as she was sniffing. They imitated everything she did. It was how they learned. It was how they survived in a world that would, if they were not wary, end their young lives as abruptly and mercilessly as they ended the lives of so many other creatures.

Spurred by curiosity and an empty belly, the female grunted and headed down a timbered slope toward the valley floor. She moved with the shuffling gait of all her kind, her hairy body flowing over the ground with an ease and economy of movement that belied her bulk.

She was big, this female. More than five feet from the tip of her nose to the tip of her bushy tail. She weighed more than fifty pounds, which was more than most females, yet less than the huge male she had mated with. Her dark eyes gleamed with vitality and intelligence. Her teeth were razors, her curved claws could rend flesh and bone as if they were clay. She was in the prime of her life and her power, the queen of her vast wilderness domain.

Of all the animals in the wild, her kind were the most fearless. The female had never known a moment of fright her whole life. She was afraid of nothing, not the giant bears she occasionally ran into or the big cats that were wont to dispute her passage or the wolves that tried to steal her caches. It was always *she* who sent *them* running. For sheer, unbridled ferocity, she had no equal. Only others like her could match her, and only the huge male could best her.

Fearlessly she lived, and fearlessly she now descended toward the strange scents and equally strange lights at several points along the shore of the lake at the center of the valley.

The female had not been down to the lake in two winters. She had no need. Her thirst was slaked by various streams that meandered from the snowy heights to feed the lake. Prey was plentiful year-round. The high forests were her usual haunts, not the more open ground below.

She came to a rock outcropping and stepped to the edge. Silhouetted against the stars, she raised her head and sniffed. The scents were stronger. Scents of animals she had never smelled. Scents of animals that could fill her empty belly and the empty bellies of her five shadows.

She glanced back at them. Like her, they were nearly invisible in the night. Their eyesight was not exceptional, not like their sense of smell and their keen ears, but still they were used to the dark, and she could see them as clearly as if the sun were up. Two were males, three were females. They had been with her almost two years. Soon she must drive them away and they would go find domains of their own, leaving her free to mate with the huge male and give birth to more young in the perpetual cycle by which she lived.

These five were her sixth litter. They had grown at a remarkable rate, so much so, the biggest male and the biggest female were almost as big as she. Keeping them fed was a challenge. She was always on the go, always on the lookout for something to eat. It helped that her kind would eat anything, from roots and berries and eggs to any animal they could catch.

Some creatures, like the big cats, were faster, and some, like the elk, were many times larger; yet none—not even the most clever of foxes or the wiliest of coyotes—could surpass her kind in raw cunning.

Ferocity and cunning. Along with tenacity, they defined all that she and those like her were. She lived to kill. In all the mountains, in all the wilderness, her kind were the most efficient slayers to be found. Most other creatures fled at the merest whiff of her musk.

Accustomed as she was to always inspiring fear in others, and never having felt it herself, it did not occur to the female that the strange lights and the strange scents presented any danger to her or her brood. The lights and scents were new, they were different, they should be investigated, as would any potential source of food.

Still, when the female came to the valley floor, she slowed and stalked warily forward. New sounds reached her keen ears, puzzling sounds she could not explain.

Sounds so alien, they raised the hackles on her neck and filled her with an uncharacteristic unease.

Where once the shore of the lake had been flat and bare, there now stood three giant piles of logs. They reminded the female of the mounds beaver lived in, only these were many times larger and had sharp angles. One was at the west end of the lake, another midway along the south shore, the third midway along the north. Their purpose eluded her. The light came from glowing squares lit with a radiance unlike the pale gleam of the moon or starlight.

From inside the nearest pile of wood came a peculiar chattering. The female could not compare it to anything in her experience. It was like the chatter of chipmunks, only fuller and louder and punctuated now and again by high brittle squeals. Something was in there. Something alive.

At the moment, though, the female was more interested in a number of large creatures that milled about to one side of the nearest log den. She slunk closer and realized they were hemmed by slim logs laid end to end, with gaps between. The creatures were somewhat like elk in their general shape and as tall as elk at the shoulder, but these had long flowing hair on their necks, which elk did not have, and long flowing tails, and the sounds they made were not sounds elk made.

Still, they were prey, and the female stalked toward them with her body slung low to the ground.

Suddenly light spilled from the pile of logs. A large hole had opened, a rectangle ablaze like the sun, and out strode one of the noisy creatures from inside, holding a long stick. The creature moved to where the elk-like animals were milling about and made a series of sounds that calmed them. Then the creature turned and stared in the direction of the female and her offspring.

The female was not concerned. She was too far from the light for the new creature to see her. She noted how it came slowly forward and raised the long stick, and she sensed a significance to the long stick that was beyond her ken. She also sensed one of her brood stir, and she hissed so only he heard and knew to stay where he was or suffer her wrath.

The strange one stopped. The female was tempted to attack, but just then another of the strange creatures came out of the log den. This one was shorter and slender and had long flowing hair, like the tails of the elk-like animals. It, too, carried a long stick, and it made a noise that caused the first one to turn and walk over to it.

Then a third creature emerged, the smallest yet, with flowing hair like the second. The three of them made many sounds until the large one motioned and all three went back inside the pile of logs and the rectangle of light blinked out.

Bewilderment gripped the female. This was alien and oddly disturbing. She started to turn to lead her offspring back up into the high country. She froze when yet another new scent reached her quivering nostrils. It came from a smaller pile of logs situated a short distance away. It was a bird scent, but birds unlike any with which the female was familiar.

She crept closer. From within came soft clucks and the flapping of wings. She sniffed and scratched at one of the logs, and the clucking grew louder. The birds had heard her and were scared.

The female circled the logs, seeking a way in. A recessed hole held promise, but it was blocked by a flat piece of wood. She pressed against it but it would not budge, so she used her claws. The birds uttered frightened squawks.

Maybe it was the racket they made. Or maybe it was the stomping of the elk-like animals that brought the largest of the strange creatures back outside, this time holding a long stick in one hand and a glowing object in the other.

Light spread across the grass toward the female. In three bounds she darted around the small pile of logs and was crouched in deep darkness beside her young ones. The strange creature came closer. The light brightened but it did not touch the female or her shadows.

The strange creature bent toward the pile, then straightened and raised the glowing object up high.

The female girded to attack, but the strange creature retraced its steps to the rectangle of light and the light went out.

A pang in the female's belly galvanized her into going around the side of the logs and renewing her assault on the flat piece of wood. She liked juicy bird meat, whether it was duck or the succulent geese that came to the valley twice a year or the occasional grouse.

Her claws did their work. The wood came away in bits and pieces. Within moments she had gouged a slit, and through it came the bird scent, strong as could be. In her famished state it was enough to drive the female into a frenzy. She threw herself at the barrier as if she had gone amok, her teeth and claws digging deep. Slivers flew every which way. One pierced her paw but she did not stop. It was a trifling discomfort. She could endure worse.

One of her young growled. She did not think to wonder why, and the next moment light washed over her. Belatedly, she realized what that meant and whirled. Thunder boomed. Something struck a log next to her with a loud *thwack*, and an acrid odor assailed her.

Two of the strange creatures had come outside, the large one and the slender one with flowing hair. Wisps of smoke rose from the end of the long stick held by the creature with the flowing hair.

The female screeched a challenge and flung herself at them. Quick as she was, the large strange creature was quicker. It raised its long stick, and again the female heard a clap like thunder. Simultaneously, a tremendous blow nearly buckled her forelegs out from under her. She recovered her balance but instead of charging she spun and loped into the night.

Instinct propelled her. The instinct to stay alive. She was hurt, badly hurt. Her insides churned, and she felt hot and wet and uncommonly weak. She had to concentrate to keep her legs moving. Her body wanted to lie down and rest.

Dimly, the female was conscious of the patter of her young. She heard a bellow from the large strange creature, and another clap of thunder, but she was spared another of those mysterious blows.

The female ran until she came to the base of a wooded slope. Plunging into the vegetation, she stopped to check on her brood. They were all there.

A commotion broke out along the lake but she paid it no heed. She was in too much pain to care. She was bleeding, and her left foreleg and much of her front was soaked. The blood flowed from a hole about the size of a large acorn. She licked it and tasted the salty tang she so loved. But this was her life's blood, not that of prey.

She climbed rapidly toward the high forest and her den. There she would be safe.

An unusual urgency gripped her. An overpowering need, like the need she felt when it was time to mate, or the need she felt to secret herself when it was time to give birth.

Her young ones followed, as they always did. The scent of her blood agitated them and they made more noise than they ordinarily would. The biggest of the males would not stop growling. Normally she would silence him but now she needed all her strength and focus to keep moving.

Queasiness came over her. Bitter bile rose in her gorge but the female swallowed it and kept on climbing. She thought only of her den, her haven, the sanctuary where she had raised her litters. She must get there, and get there quickly, and nothing must stand in her way.

Presently, though, the female found it hard to breathe. Her lungs strained for air. In great gulps she sought to fill them. But gradually her limbs grew numb. She lost all feeling except for the pain. The bleeding had stopped, but she suffered bouts where her mind spun, relieved by periods of clarity.

Dimly, the female perceived that her offspring were on each side of her and not behind her as they should be. The largest of the females nudged her and whined deep in her throat.

They were confused by the blood and her weakness, and did not know what to do.

She was only halfway to the high country when her strength, once so prodigious, gave out. Her stamina, once without limit, dwindled to nothing. She was empty inside, empty and cold and exhausted. For another dozen yards she staggered on, spurred by a spark in the wellspring of her being. Then her legs gave out and she collapsed in an exhausted sprawl.

Her brood was all around her, licking, nipping, whining, urging, but all she could do was lie there, unable to respond or move. She tried to test the wind for enemies, but she could not raise her head high enough. She was helpless, totally and completely helpless, and she sensed that just as she had seen the life ebb in countless prey, so was hers about to end.

All things died. It was the basic law of the wild. Most things were eaten by other things. Plants were eaten by plant eaters and the plant eaters were eaten by meat eaters and the meat eaters were eaten by other meat eaters. On and on and on it went in an endless circle of slay to survive.

The female's eating days were over. She felt her young ones nestle against her and was grateful for their warmth. The night blackened, and the next she knew, she was awake and bright sunlight hurt her eyes. She was able to raise her head enough to establish that she was lying in the open, and she was alone. Her brood had left her.

The female sank back down and closed her eyes. She was so tired. She wanted to sleep but a persistent clattering from below warned her that a creature of some kind was climbing toward her, something big, with hard hooves that rang on rock.

With a supreme effort she twisted her neck and beheld her doom.

There were two of them, the large one with the long stick and another much like him. They were astride the creatures that were like elk but were not elk. She watched them approach. She saw them point their long sticks when they spotted her, and then lower the sticks again.

Slowly, cautiously, they came closer. The large one from the night before, whose scent the female recognized, leaned down and made sounds. The other, younger and slightly smaller, showed its teeth and pointed its long stick.

The female heard a sound like the snapping of a dry twig. She thought of her five young ones and the joy they had brought her. She thought of the valley that had once been hers and was now theirs, and these strange intruders with their log dens and long sticks that spat death. She thought how wonderful it would be if her young ones did to the intruders as the intruders were about to do to her.

Then came another crash of thunder that was not thunder, and the female knew nothing, absolutely nothing at all.

CHAPTER ONE

Winona King was in paradise.

She liked that word, paradise. Many of the words the whites used had so many meanings, it was hard sometimes to choose the right one. But paradise, so far as she knew, had only one meaning. Her husband had defined it as a place of bliss where everyone was happy. That certainly fit. Winona was as happy as she could ever recall being, with ample and sufficient reasons.

First, Winona loved their new home. The valley was everything she dared hope it would be: verdant, beautiful, ringed by majestic peaks, abundant with animal life, a Garden of Eden, as Nate called it, only without the serpent. That last allusion puzzled her since she had come across a number of snakes since they got there, including several rattlers. Then she realized he was referring to the serpent from the Bible.

Second, Winona loved being close to her son and his

wife. Before, Zach and Louisa had lived so far away she was lucky to see them once a moon, if that. Now she need only walk to the north side of the lake. Since they built their new cabins, she had spent many a wonderful hour sipping tea and talking to Lou. Zach, though, was seldom home. He was always off hunting or exploring. But she still saw him more often than she had before, and that was something.

Third, Winona loved being near Shakespeare McNair and his Flathead mate, Blue Water Woman. They were her best friends, and she delighted in their companionship.

Fourth, and this was perhaps the most important reason of all, her daughter liked it there. Liked it enough that Evelyn no longer talked about leaving and going back East to live. Part of that had to do with her terrible experiences on their last trip to the States, but part of it, an important part, had to do with the indisputable fact that at long, long last, Evelyn was learning to appreciate the wilderness she so long abhorred.

It had always worried and upset Winona, her daughter's loathing of the mountains and everything in them. Time without end, Evelyn had complained that it was stupid to live in the Rockies when they never knew from one day to the next if they would be alive to greet the next dawn.

Evelyn had always hankered to head East, to live where she need not fear walking out the door. "I don't need hostiles in my life, thank you very much," she once commented to Winona. "Or grizzlies or painters or whatever else might take a notion to eat me."

Winona had tried to explain that there was more to life in the wild than the dangers. She sought to impress on Evelyn that the beauty and the grandeur more than made up for the perils, but it was always the perils Evelyn harped on, to the point where Evelyn had convinced herself it was outright lunacy to live west of the Mississippi.

But now Evelyn was having second thoughts. She had not completely changed her mind, but she was open to the possibility that the mountains offered more than she used to admit. That alone, in Winona's estimation, was cause for celebration, because the truth be known, she very much wanted her daughter to stay.

Winona loved her children dearly. Having them both there in the new valley filled her with immense pleasure. She got to see them; she was able to help them if they needed it. Life was perfect.

Now, stepping out of her cabin into the bright gleam of the new day, Winona drew up short. The love of her life was hunkered in front of the chicken coop, picking at the coop door with a fingernail. Smoothing her beaded buckskin dress, she walked over. "Will it need to be replaced, husband?" she asked in her impeccable English.

Nate King shifted on the heels of his moccasins. "Afraid so. But I have a few boards left from when we put in our floor. It won't take but two shakes of an antelope's tail."

"It was brazen of the wolverine to try and eat our chickens." Winona was glad it had not succeeded. Only recently had they bartered for six hens and a rooster from emigrants on a wagon train bound for Oregon Country, and it was a treat to have fresh eggs every morning.

"Gluttons are worse than grizzlies," Nate com-

13

mented. Dreaded by white and red men alike, the Skunk Bear, as wolverines were also nicknamed, was widely considered to be the most formidable creature on the continent. Back in the days when Nate made his living as a trapper, gluttons had been the scourge of the trapping fraternity. The beasts raided trap lines, ripping the beaver from the steel jaws that held them fast. Many a trapper had gone out to check his line, only to find every trap sprung, with strips of flesh and hair all that remained of the prized plew that would add coins to the trapper's purse. Nate had lost more than a few beaver himself to roving gluttons, and it always left him fuming mad.

"There are far more grizzlies than wolverines," Winona was saying. "But now that you have killed it, we need not fear a return visit."

"Zach was the one who shot it." Nate had intended to, but the sight of the wolverine lying there in a pool of blood, with red rivulets oozing from its nose and mouth, had stayed his trigger finger. He let his son ride up and finish the job.

"He wanted the hide," Winona said. "He has been promising Louisa a rug for months."

"All's well that ends well, then, fair Ophelia," said a new voice, and around the corner of their cabin ambled a white-haired mountain man dressed as Nate was in buckskins, with an ammo pouch, powder horn and possibles bag slanted across his chest, a brace of pistols wedged under his wide leather belt, and a Hawken rifle in his hand.

"Shakespeare!" Winona said in delight. Taking his calloused hands in hers, she pecked him on his wizened cheek. "To what do we owe this honor?"

"Lou was over to our place and told us about your visitor," Shakespeare McNair answered. "I reckoned I'd come over to check on your chickens." He turned to the coop and quoted in greeting, "Good my Lord, how does your honor for this many a day?"

"If you're asking me what I think you're asking me," Nate responded, "I'm doing right fine. How about you?"

"Excellent well," Shakespeare answered, and grinned. "You are a fishmonger, I see."

"Don't start."

"Good my Lord, what is your cause of distemper?"

"There you go again," Nate groused. "Talking that nonsense no one understands and doesn't want to. One of these days you will talk plain English like the rest of us and the shock will keel me over."

McNair took a step back, his hand to his throat, and flushed from his neck to his hairline. "*What* did you just say? Did my ears perceive correctly? Did you insult the *Bard?*"

"I might have," Nate said. "One of us isn't in love with him."

Sputtering, Shakespeare looked at Winona and then back at Nate, and in grand eloquent fashion demanded, "Is this the thanks I get for taking you under my wing when you were as green as grass? Is this how you express your gratitude for the years I've spent molding you into a frontiersman worthy of his powder? You heap abuse on genius far removed from our shallow brains?"

Nate smiled innocently up at him. "Who would that be, again? James Fenimore Cooper?"

Shakespeare looked fit to bust a blood vessel. "I shall laugh myself to death at this puppy-headed monster! A

15

most scurvy monster! I could find it in my heart to beat him!"

"Did he just call me a puppy?" Nate asked Winona.

"There's no more faith in thee than in a stewed prune!" Shakespeare fumed. "You know the Bard is my only earthly idol. You know I have a dog-eared copy of his works and committed to memory many of his marvelous truths. How dare you insult old William S.! How prove you that in the great heap of your knowledge?"

Nate unfurled and stretched. As always, his mentor's mock outrage never failed to amuse. At least he hoped it was mock. "All right. I admit defeat. William Shakespeare was the greatest scribbler who ever drew breath."

"Scribbler?" Shakespeare repeated. "That's like saying Michelangelo dabbled in paint."

"He didn't?"

Shakespeare blinked and laughed, and Nate joined in the mirth. "You are a tribute to my taunts, young coon."

Winona breathed deep of the crisp mountain air. Here was yet another example of why she loved their new home so much. "Have you two ever noticed that you act more like five-year-olds than grown men?"

"Was she talking to us?" Shakespeare asked.

"It's best if we ignore her," Nate said.

"You do," Winona warned, "and that wolverine will seem tame compared to what I will do."

"Ah, yes, the *carcajou*," Shakespeare said, using the French name. "I hear it had a hankering for chicken." He examined the claw and teeth marks. "Your son tells me it was as big as a griz."

Winona snickered. "Our son enjoys telling tall tales, like his father." She bobbed her chin toward the lake.

"Remember that fish he caught? The one that was longer than his leg?"

"It was," Nate insisted. He had caught it on a bone hook and after ten minutes of fierce struggle, the hook snapped.

Shakespeare winked at Winona. "Have I ever told you, my dear, about the time I came across a butterfly as big as a buffalo? I jumped on its back and flew around for a spell. Got as far as the Great Salt Lake and then it brought me back."

"It should have dumped you in," Nate said.

Winona chuckled and made for the cabin. "I will put a fresh pot of coffee on, and a slice of pie, besides."

"We'll be in soon," Nate promised, and undid the small metal latch to the chicken coop door. The moment he opened it, out strutted the rooster, trailed by his harem. "And a cock-a-doodle-do to you," Nate said.

"My wife wanted me to thank you again for the eggs Winona gave us," Shakespeare said. "There's nothing better than a pemmican omelette to start the day." He idly moved to the side of the coop, his gaze fixed on the lake. "How about if we go fishing later today? I'd sure like to catch one of those giant fish of yours." Smirking, he glanced down, and stopped dead. "Hallo? What's this?"

"What's what?"

"You'd best take a gander for yourself, Horatio. If it was rabbits I wouldn't bring it to your attention."

Nate walked over. "Even when you speak plain English you don't make any sense." He chortled, then felt the skin on the nape of his neck prickle. "I'll be damned."

"The one you killed was female, was it not?"

17

"So Zach said." Nate sank onto his left knee and lightly touched his hand to an impression in the dirt.

"I suppose you didn't bother to check if she was nursing?" Shakespeare shook his head at their lapse and squatted beside his surrogate son. "How many do you make it out to be?"

"Hard to say," Nate responded. Few of the prints were clear; most were a jumble. "If I had to guess, I'd peg it as three."

"Possibly four," Shakespeare said, tapping a partial track a few feet from the rest. "That fits for a good-sized litter." He traced the outline of one of the clearer prints with a fingernail. "Look at the size of this one. These aren't newborns. A year or more old, I reckon."

"Four wolverines," Nate said, and felt unaccountably, briefly, cold. "And they were here with her the whole time. They might even have seen Zach finish her off."

A minute of silence ended with Shakespeare saying, "It could be you've put the fear of man into them. It could be they'll avoid us from here on out."

"Or it could be," Nate said slowly, "they'll come back to take up where their mother left off. Or worse."

"Leave it to you to always look at the bright side," Shakespeare said, but his tone lacked his customary humor. "To put your mind at rest, maybe a hunt is in order."

"I'd rather not."

Shakespeare squinted at him. "Don't tell me. Does this have anything to do with your recent hare-brained notion to spread love and togetherness throughout the animal kingdom?"

Nate chose not to reply.

Sighing long and loud, Shakespeare stood and leaned

against the coop. "I understand. Truly I do. You're sick of the bloodshed. All the beaver you trapped, all the game you've shot, all the bears you've tangled with and all the hostiles who were out for your hair, that's a heap of killing. I savvy completely. But if you turn the other cheek out here"—McNair gestured at the towering mountains—"you end up with your face ripped off or your throat slit." He waited, and when Nate did not say anything, he asked, "Didn't you learn your lesson with that silver-tip?"

Not long afer they moved into their new cabins, a grizzly had terrorized them. Nate had tried to spare it. He did all he could to avoid a clash, but the griz saw them as food and would not relent short of hot lead.

"I take it you haven't?" Shakespeare sounded disappointed. "You do unbend your noble strength, to think so brainsickly of things," he quoted.

"I don't want to repeat past mistakes," Nate said. "I don't want to kill everything off here like I did in the last valley."

"You had to protect your loved ones. You had to eat. Feeding a family of four takes a lot of hunting."

"Granted," Nate said, "but when we left, there weren't but a few deer and elk and grouse and a porcupine or two in the whole valley. I had to ride twenty miles sometimes to find game for the cooking pot. In the old days I wouldn't have to go more than a mile or two."

"Have it your way." Shakespeare shrugged. "What do I know? Maybe the she-glutton's brats will let you be. Maybe they learned *their* lesson when you killed their ma. Maybe they won't come after your chickens." He paused meaningfully. "Or anything or anyone else."

CHAPTER TWO

Evelyn King did not like being fourteen. She did not like being, as Shakespeare McNair called it, with that flowery way with words he had, at the "cusp of womanhood." She did not like it in part because a lot of terrible things had happened to her in the past year. She had been kidnapped by a woman out for revenge against her family, and the ordeal the woman put her through had changed her outlook on life. Before that fateful day, Evelyn had always thought the best of people. She assumed they were good and decent until they proved otherwise. Now she was suspicious of everyone until they proved they deserved her trust. She would not make the same mistake twice.

The other part of her discontent was more personal. It had to do with that "womanhood" business. Much to her amazement, and considerable dismay, she was being courted by a young Crow and a young Ute. Both wanted to take her as their wife. Both wanted her to come live with their people and be a mother to their children.

The mere notion scared Evelyn near witless. She had never given much thought to being a wife and mother. Until her kidnapping, she had never thought about men in *that* way. Given her druthers, she would rather not think about them *that* way for a good long while yet.

Now, strolling thoughtfully along the lake shore, her hands clasped behind her back, Evelyn pondered her dilemma and the state of affairs in general.

Evelyn was dressed in a blue homespun dress she made herself. Blue was her favorite color. She loved the velvet blue of the sky and the rich, deep blue of the lake hinting at bottomless depths; she loved the vivid blue of the forget-me-not flowers that bloomed above the timberline late in the summer. The pattern for her dress came from a catalog her father brought from St. Louis. It was filled with delightful wonders, from clothes to hair brushes to items for the home and the kitchen.

It was always Evelyn's dream to live back East and own everything in that catalog and to have a nice house to put all those nice things in. In other words, to live in a civilized fashion.

Evelyn never liked the wilderness. She could do without the hardships. She could do without enemy war parties, rattlesnakes, grizzlies and mountain lions. She could do without everything that made life in the wilds so fraught with danger.

Until she was kidnapped, Evelyn regarded civilized life as heaven on earth, as the ideal way for people to live. But that image had been tarnished. Civilization, she learned the hard way, was not the idyllic bliss she imagined. Like the wilderness, it had a dark underside, elements so vile, so hideous, they were hidden from sight in dens of iniquity.

Evelyn stopped and stared out over the lake. Her thoughts were straying. She had come outside to decide what to do about one of her suitors who was due to pay a visit soon, not to rehash the old debate of which she favored most; the untamed mountains or the orderly world of civilization.

Evelyn was about to walk on when she heard her name called. Turning, she saw her mother hurrying toward her. She knew why when she saw what her mother was holding.

"You forgot these," Winona said in annoyance. If she had told her daughter once, she had told her a thousand times not to leave the cabin without them.

"I'm only going a short way," Evelyn justified her lapse.

"Must we go through this again?" Winona responded. "Your father and I talk until our throats are hoarse but you refuse to listen. It is only common sense to take a few precautions."

To spare herself another of her mother's lectures, she accepted the Hawken, a pair of pistols and a leather belt to wedge the pistols under, and a powder horn and ammo pouch. "Thank you, but you need not have bothered."

"For someone who worries so much about bears and the like, you don't show much common sense." Winona folded her arms and waited while Evelyn armed herself. "There. Now you won't be eaten by the first meat eater that comes along, or taken by hostiles without a fight."

"We haven't seen hide nor hair of a war party since we came here."

"That doesn't mean we let down our guard." Winona smiled and placed a hand on Evelyn's shoulder. "I am happy you have come to terms with where we live but do not make the mistake of taking things for granted."

"I never do," Evelyn said, unable to hide her resentment at the reminder.

"There comes a time, daughter, when we must take responsibility for what we do."

"Don't start," Evelyn said. She did not want another talking to. She had heard it all before, many times over.

"I do not understand you sometimes," Winona said. "Just last night a wolverine tried to eat our chickens. Yet today you come out unarmed and alone and do not tell anyone where you are going." She gently squeezed Evelyn's shoulder. "Are you trying to get yourself killed?"

Evelyn grew warm with anger. "I did not tell you because I'm not going very far. Only a hundred yards or so."

"And if a mountain lion or a bear happen by?" Winona persisted. "They would run you down before you were halfway to our cabin." She waited for her daughter to say something, and when no reply was forthcoming, she turned toward their cabin. "Very well. I will not impose further."

Racked by guilt, Evelyn watched her mother's retreating figure until she went in. Then, hefting the Hawken her father had special made for her, she continued north, saying aloud, "Some things never change." Her mother meant well, but Evelyn resented being reminded of what she should and shouldn't do. She would turn fifteen in a few months, and she was perfectly capable of deciding for herself.

In a sulk, Evelyn paid little attention to what was going on around her until a loud splash startled her. She glanced at the lake but whatever made the splash was gone. A large fish, she guessed, had broken the surface. She went another thirty feet, to a boulder at the water's edge, and sat facing the water. Her father had always told her never to sit with her back to the woods, but the woods were an arrow's flight away. Besides, the mood she was in, she would like for something to try and sneak up on her just so she could shoot it.

Placing the Hawken's stock on the ground, Evelyn leaned on the rifle and bowed her head. Her emotions were making a mess of her head. She must keep them under a tight rein and work out what she would say to Chases Rabbits.

Evelyn had decided enough was enough. While it was flattering that Chases Rabbits and Niwot wanted her for their woman, she was much too young to even think about marriage. Sure, some girls her age took husbands, but she had absolutely no interest in tying herself to someone for the rest of her life. Not at—

A strange feeling came over her. Twisting, Evelyn stared toward the trees. She would swear she was being watched; she could practically feel unseen eyes on her. Her mother had advised her never to discount her intuition, as it might save her life, but although she gazed long and hard into the shadowed timber, she saw nothing to account for her feeling.

Nerves, Evelyn reasoned, after her mother's talk about grizzlies and painters and such. Chuckling at her silliness, she faced the azure lake and placed the Hawken across her lap.

Now where was she? Evelyn mused. Oh, yes; Chases Rabbits. He would be there in a few days, and she must be ready. She must be firm. She must make her wishes clear and insist he respect them.

Evelyn liked him. She truly did. But as a friend, not a potential husband. She had no interest in courting or being courted, and would sooner kiss her horse than a male. It was—

Again that strange feeling of being watched came over her. Shifting, Evelyn scanned the tree line, with the same result as before. Not so much as a bird stirred. That in itself was unusual. It struck her how silent the forest had become. Puzzled, she stood and moved toward it, the Hawken level at her waist, her thumb on the hammer. A tiny voice deep in her mind told her she was being ridiculous, that there was no cause to be concerned, that it was nerves and only nerves.

Evelyn halted twenty feet out. She did not care to get too close in case something rushed her. Mountain lions—and grizzlies, for that matter—were incredibly swift when they had a need to be. She probed every swatch of shade, every bush and under every tree, and did not spot so much as a butterfly.

Yet the sensation of being watched would not go away.

Her unease growing, Evelyn debated whether to enter the woods and root whatever it was out. She started to but changed her mind. Her Hawken was powerful enough to bring down a man or a big cat, but it would barely slow a griz. Caution dictated she not overstep herself.

Evelyn backed toward the lake. She was so intent on the forest that when something clutched at her arm, she shrieked and whirled, prepared to sell her life as dearly as a King should.

"What in blazes has you so spooked, sis?"

"Zach!" Evelyn blurted.

Zachary King was nine years her senior. Of the two of them, he most bore the stamp of their mother's heritage, both in his features and his swarthy cast, and in the Shoshone-style buckskins and style of hair he affected. Like her, he had ink-black hair and emerald green eyes. Like her, he was armed with a rifle and pistol. He also, like his father, did not go anywhere without a bowie strapped to one hip and a tomahawk on the other. "Who did you think it was? One of those handsome suitors of yours?"

Evelyn forgot about the thing in the trees. "Quit teasing me. I didn't ask them to come courting, you know."

"Females are scarce in these parts," Zach grinned, "which makes you as valuable as gold. Warts and all."

"They can't be all that scarce," Evelyn rejoined. "Even you found a wife."

Zach's grin evaporated and he squared his broad shoulders. "I'll have you know she finds me right handsome."

"Did she ever get those spectacles she needs?"

"Why, you little scamp," Zach said, and burst out laughing. "You sure can hold your own."

"I had a good teacher," Evelyn said with genuine affection. For all the barbs they traded, she adored her brother, adored him dearly. He had forever enshrined himself in her heart by saving her from her kidnapper.

"So what are you up to?" Zach asked. "I saw you over by the trees and figured you were looking to shoot some poor defenseless squirrel."

Evelyn's lips pinched together. "I won't shoot anything unless I have to. You know that. I thought I was being watched, but it was my imagination."

"Oh?" Zach's eyes narrowed. "How about we have a look-see?" He assumed she would agree and made for the greenery, his movements as lithe as a panther's. "It takes some getting used to, doesn't it, sis?"

"What does?"

"Our new valley. It's not like the old one. We were fairly safe there. Pa and me had killed off all the predators." Zach paused, and frowned. "It beats me why he's become so dead set against killing. Sometimes it has to be done."

"He's sick of it, is all," Evelyn repeated her father's justification. "You can't blame him after all the critters he's done in." She had never much liked killing, herself, but if they did not shoot game, they did not eat meat. It was that simple.

"I hope to God I don't get like him," Zach said. "A person has to do what they have to do. That's all there is to it."

Evelyn suddenly touched his arm, and stopped. "There. Do you feel that?" Her skin prickled as if she had a heat rash.

"Feel what?"

"We're being watched."

"I don't feel anything," Zach said, but he did not discount it out of hand. Experience had taught him not to. He surveyed the woodland, and his brow furrowed. "That's funny. It's as quiet as a burial ground."

"I noticed that, too."

"Stay close, little one," Zach admonished, and made for a gap in the trees. He hoped they would flush something. He loved to hunt, almost as much as he enjoyed counting coup on an enemy.

"Stop calling me that." Evelyn raised her rifle to her shoulder. She did not doubt for a moment that her brother could handle anything they encountered short of a grizzly, and her father had slain the silver-tip that once roamed the valley.

Shadows dappled the vegetation. Above, cottonwood leaves fluttered in the breeze. A patch of weeds rustled.

"Too bad one of your suitors isn't here," Zach jousted. "We could stake him out as bait."

Evelyn almost kicked him. But a loud commotion broke out in a nearby thicket, and a female grouse took wing like a feathered cannonball.

Instantly Zach pivoted, tracking the bird with his cheek tucked to his Hawken. His finger curled around the trigger.

"Don't," Evelyn said.

For a few seconds Zach did not move or speak. The grouse disappeared among a cluster of pines, and he reluctantly lowered his rifle. "If Lou and I go hungry tonight, it's your fault. That was a mighty plump bird."

"You have plenty of venison left from that buck you shot two days ago," Evelyn reminded him.

Zach studied the ground for sign. It was covered by a carpet of leaves and pine needles, and the only tracks that would show clearly were those of heavy animals like elk and deer and bear. He moved past a maple. In its shade grew a shootingstar, as some called it, and there, stuck to the long, slender leaves at the base of the stalk, was a clump of short, fine, dark brown hairs. Stooping, he pulled the cluster off and held it in the palm of his hand.

"What do you have there?" Evelyn asked.

Zach sniffed the clump, scowled, and held his hand out to her. "It wasn't your imagination."

Evelyn bent and sniffed. "I don't smell anything."

"Try again, lunkhead," Zach said, and practically shoved the hairs up her nose.

Evelyn recoiled. The foul musk was faint but potent. "Is this what I think it is?"

Zach grimly nodded. "You were being watched, all right, little sister. By a wolverine."

CHAPTER THREE

Four of the five were bewildered by their mother's death. They had seen many animals die; they had killed many themselves. But it never occurred to them on the almost purely instinctual level on which they functioned, that their mother would suffer the same fate.

Only the largest male was unaffected. Like the rest, he watched from concealment as the strange creature pointed a long stick at his mother. He heard a mysterious blast and witnessed his mother's skull erupt in a shower of fur, bone and brains. He saw the strange creature climb down off the four-legged elk-like animal, and with an effort lift his mother's body and throw it over the four-leg, which shied and would have run off had the strange creature not held on to a vine that dangled from the four-leg's neck.

No sooner were his mother's killers out of sight than the male padded to where his mother had lain and sniffed at the pool of blood. She was gone, gone forever. He knew that as surely as he knew anything. The five of them were on their own.

The others came out of hiding and gathered around. The biggest female brushed against him and the big male growled. He did not like them so close. They were his sisters and brothers but he suddenly felt an urge to be by himself.

The big female was staring at him. The male met her stare, then turned and melted into the forest. He never glanced back. He did not have a special destination in mind. He wanted only to get away from the others.

Unthinkingly, the male headed down the mountain instead of up. The lights far below reminded him of the strange slayers, and he grew hot despite the chill of the night air. The male did not know what he would do when he got there. He just needed to go.

The den in which he had been raised was not far above, but the male would never visit it again. With his mother gone there was no need.

The lights went out long before he came to the valley floor. He prowled near the pile of logs his mother had visited but he did not go as close as she had. He had learned from her mistake. The strange ones were dangerous. They had long sticks that killed. He must avoid them. He must keep on going and leave the valley and find another of his own.

Instead, the male stood and stared at one of the log dens in which the strange ones lived. He would like to sink his teeth into one of them, to rip and rend until the strange one was no more, like his mother. Until the strange one was dead, dead, dead.

The big male looped wide of the log den and went

into the vegetation to the west of the water. For the rest of the night he hunted, flushing a rabbit at one point and a small doe later. He killed both. The rabbit he devoured in a few great bites but the doe was more than he could consume so he marked the remains by spraying it with musk and kicking a few leaves and sticks over it. Then he went into the undergrowth near the water and curled up in a thicket to sleep.

The male did not awaken until the sun was high in the sky. He stretched and started to rise then flattened and slunk to where he had a better view of a strange one tramping north at the water's edge. Apparently the noisy ones came in all sizes. This one was smaller than the others.

The male studied it and was considerably taken aback when it unexpectedly stopped and gazed in his direction.

The male was well hidden. He could not fathom how the strange creature knew he was there. He tensed when it came toward him and pointed a long stick. But the stick did not make thunder. Before long the strange creature was close enough that the male's sensitive nose registered its scent.

Something about the smell impressed on the male that this particular strange one was female. He fought down an impulse to burst from the forest and rip her to pieces. Not so long as she held a long stick.

Presently a second strange one appeared, and they chattered. Surprise nearly cost the young male his life, for when the pair came toward the woods, he lay frozen in place until they were much too close. As it was, he snuck away unnoticed but it required all the stealth he possessed. With every step, he was tensed for the blast of a long stick and the searing explosion of his skull.

They did not spot him, though.

The larger of the two found some of his hair, and after more chattering, the pair headed for the log den to the south. The male let them go. He would bide his time. All creatures let their vigilance lapse, and the male would very much like to be within pouncing distance of a strange one when the strange one did not have a long stick.

Careful not to be seen, the male kept them in sight. Patience was called for, a trait for which his kind were noted. Eventually he would have his way; eventually he would feast on one of the strange creatures as he would on any other animal.

His mouth watered in anticipation.

The big female did not try to stop the biggest male from leaving. She felt no special tie to him. He had been a den mate and her brother but now that their mother was gone, they were on their own. She turned to go up the mountain and only went a short way when she realized the other three were following her.

Stopping, she glanced back. They stopped, too. They were looking at her with the same eager expectance they had shown toward their mother, and she divined in some indefinable manner that she had taken her mother's place. She bared her teeth to snarl and drive them off but on an impulse she made the same soft low cry her mother always made to reassure them, and resumed climbing. They trotted close behind.

The female was hungry, but food could wait. She was

making for their den. Only there would she and the others be safe.

Their mother had chosen well. The den was in a crevice above the tree line. It was barely wide enough for them to slip inside, and much too narrow for a grizzly or a black bear. On one side was an overhang that sheltered them from rain and snow and the worst of the wind. Mountain lions and wolves could get at them, but only from the front, and only by lunging under the overhang, thereby exposing their necks.

The female lay on her belly in the spot her mother always occupied. Her siblings sprawled nearby, the small male mewing over their loss. He was the only male left. The other two were females. They were bigger than he was, although not as big as the biggest female, and nearly identical in appearance; one had a lighter band of hair in front of her ears.

The three of them slept but the biggest female could not. She lay with her muzzle on her forepaws and closed her eyes, but rest eluded her. Conflicting urges tore at her like rapids in a mountain stream. She wanted to leave. She wanted to stay. She wanted to be by herself. She wanted to be with the others. Most of all, she wanted her mother, and somehow it comforted her to be lying where her mother had so often lain and to smell her mother's lingering scent.

Time crawled on a snail's back. Dawn was not far off when the female stirred, rose on all fours and grunted as her mother always grunted to awaken the others. She was out of the crevice and padding toward the forest before they caught up.

Hunger dominated her. Her kind needed to eat, and eat frequently.

She repeatedly tested the air. More than her eyes or even her ears, she relied on her nose the most. She could smell prey from a long distance off. Much farther than a bear could, or a wolf or a coyote. Her nose was the sharpest of all the creatures that roamed the mountains. To her the world was a complex mosaic of odors her nose deciphered with ease.

Now the breeze brought the big female a familiar scent. Elk were below. Not one or two but a herd in dense timber bordering a meadow. The herd was composed entirely of cows. The bulls would not join them until rutting season.

The female had been to the meadow before and knew of a gully that would conceal her and her siblings until they were near enough to pounce.

As silently as gliding owls, the four hairy hunters slunk lower. The female stopped when she heard the soft call of a cow. Flattening, she stalked to the gully's rim and peered over it.

Eight cows and four calves were drifting toward the meadow. Elk routinely grazed at dawn and dusk. Afterward, they always retired into the depths of the forest and slept the day away.

The female ignored the cows. They were too large and too strong to bring down. Calves, though, were weak and slow, and one was plodding along in its mother's wake quite near the gully.

Suddenly the mother raised her head, sniffed, and uttered a barking snort. The danger cry. Wheeling, she bolted to the south. The other cows and calves immediately did the same.

A long bound carried the big female out of the gully. She was not as fast as the elk but over a short distance she could overtake them before they gained enough speed to elude her.

The calf squealed as the female came alongside. Eyes wide in terror, it veered to escape, but she glued herself to it like a second shadow.

Another squeal caused the mother to slow. She began to turn to come to her offspring's aid.

The female knew she must accomplish her goal before the cow reached her. She did not fear the cow, but neither did she care to risk broken bones from the cow's flailing hoofs. Mouth agape, she sprang. Her teeth sheared through soft flesh, severing a vein, and warm blood moistened her head and neck as she clamped her iron jaws and wrenched with all her might.

Squawking hysterically, the calf tumbled head over tail. A bony leg caught the female hard across the ribs, but she did not slacken her hold.

Suddenly the cow was there. Snorting in fury, she sought to stomp the female with her heavy hooves, but the female twisted aside. Frantic, the cow kicked at the big female's head and missed.

Other cows converged. The female was about to be stomped to death in a furious frenzy, but the next instant the wolverine's sisters and brother were among the elk, snapping and snarling.

In desperation the mother lowered her head and butted at the big female, but her brother leaped between them, his claws raking the cow from her ear to her eyes. One of her sisters snapped at the cow's legs. The cow had no recourse but to flee, bawling in misery.

By then the calf was barely moving. The big female lay across it, worrying the jugular. Gnashing and rend-ing, she savored the rich wet blood that flowed down her gullet.

The rest of the herd crashed through the undergrowth in panicked flight. They would not stop until they were exhausted.

The two sisters and the brother tore at the calf. It was not yet dead, but in deep shock. When the male bit down on the calf's face, ripping off a cheek and one eyeball, it bleated loudly and shrilly, and then finally was still.

Now came the best part: the feast. The big female sucked on the jugular until the calf's lifeblood dwindled to a trickle. She tore at the soft flesh, savoring the deliciously sweet meat. When the male came too near, she snapped at him, biting him, but not deep enough to cause serious harm.

They gorged until the sun was directly overhead. Sated and content, the quartet lazed in the sunlight.

For a while the female forgot about her mother and the strange creatures that killed her. She forgot about the three mouths depending on her. She dozed, and might have slept the rest of the day away had the male not growled and the two smaller females not stood up and hissed like a pair of bobcats.

Then the scent reached her, and the big female rose and glowered at the intruder lumbering deliberately toward them and what was left of their meal.

A full-grown black bear, every whit as powerful as two of her kind combined, had its huge head tilted back, and was noisily sniffing. It was being drawn to the aroma of fresh blood as it would be to honey.

The four stood their ground, bristling fiercely. It was

against their nature to relinquish a kill. Although they were young and inexperienced, they would perish before they gave up the calf's remains.

For a while a stalemate prevailed. The black bear growled and blustered and clawed furrows in the ground. The four siblings snarled and hissed and gnashed their teeth.

Ultimately, the black bear decided the numbers were not in his favor, and with as much ursine dignity as he could muster, he barreled off into the vegetation, an ambulatory avalanche plowing through everything in its path.

The confrontation had rekindled the big female's hunger. She settled down to finish what was left and was joined by her siblings. Gnawed bones and bits and tufts were scattered about when they eventually rose and wound up the gully to the high slopes and the crevice.

Another day almost gone.

The first of their new life.

They laid up only until sunset. Shrouded by twilight, the big female led them out of the den and along the crest of a ridge to a shelf overlooking the valley.

Far below glowed the lights of the strange ones. The female would like to pay them another visit. Curiosity had a lot to do with it, but so did the most basic tenet of her existence: All creatures were potential prey. From the largest to the smallest, whether fur clad or covered with features or scales, they were food for her belly, and her belly came before all else.

The big female started down the mountain. Since the others did whatever she did, they followed. In single file they descended slope after slope.

The big female wanted to see the strange ones again.

Presently she crossed the trail of a familiar scent and stopped. She ran her nose over the ground to confirm it. Her biggest brother had passed that way sometime during the night. He was bound for the valley floor, too. Perhaps to the giant log piles of the strange ones.

The female moved on. Her curiosity and her belly would not be denied. Just as she had cleverly and efficiently ended the calf's life, so would she end the lives of her mother's slayers.

Every last one.

CHAPTER FOUR

Shakespeare McNair did not let on to his wife or Nate King or Nate's wife or Nate's son or daughter or Louisa King, but he was worried. Extremely worried. More worried than he had been in ten coon's ages, and that took some doing. For out of all of them, Shakespeare knew exactly what wolverines were capable of. He'd had more dealings with the legendary gluttons, back when he initially came to the Rockies.

Shakespeare had been the first. The very first. Before any of the rest. Before Lewis and Clark, before Bridger, before Carson, before Smith. He was the first American to cross the mile-wide Mississippi River and the many-miles-wide prairie and set eyes on the mile-high snow-crowned ramparts that would become his home for the rest of his days.

Young and green and without a prejudiced bone in his body, Shakespeare had taken up Indian ways. He ate what they ate, wore the same clothes they wore. He fought their enemies, both human and bestial, including Skunk Bears.

Shakespeare liked to tease Nate about all the times Nate had tangled with grizzlies, but if the truth were known, Shakespeare had tangled with gluttons almost as many times as Nate had with bears, so much so, he was called Carcajou, or Wolverine, by various tribes.

Shakespeare learned about gluttons fast. He had to. The first one he ran up against seemed to take perverse delight in raiding his traps day after day, depriving him of the furry fruits of his hard labor. He tried to track it to its lair, but the wolverine was clever and did not leave sign. He tried to poison it, but the wolverine never ate the tainted bait. So in desperation he sat up in a tree one night and when, along about dawn, he heard grunts and growls and the crunch of bones, he beheld a wolverine for the very first time—devouring a beaver caught in one of his traps.

Shakespeare shot it. He saw it drop, and assuming it was dead, he climbed down to examine the body. Only the glutton was very much alive and it came at him like a demented demon, clawing and biting and savagely determined to inflict the same pain on him that he had inflicted on it.

Over the decades Shakespeare had battled many foes of all different kinds, but it was safe to state that his battle that morning with the enraged wolverine on the bank of a stream that did not yet have a name was one of the two or three most fierce battles of his entire long and tumultuous life.

Shakespeare, as was his habit, had reloaded right after firing. He got off another shot as the wolverine rushed him and scored a clear hit to the wolverine's shoulder, but it did not even slow the wolverine down. Shakespeare had grabbed for his knife, and the glutton was on him.

How he survived, Shakespeare would never rightly know. The wolverine had been immensely strong. Pound for pound for their size, they were the strongest animal alive. Somehow Shakespeare had gotten a forearm under its bottom jaw to keep its awful teeth from shredding his flesh like so much cheese, and he had stabbed and stabbed and stabbed, thrusting his blade again and again into the bulky body until his arm throbbed from the exertion.

Just when Shakespeare thought the beast was indestructible, it collapsed on top of him.

His second clash occurred when Shakespeare lived with the Flatheads. Something had been coming around the village at night, helping itself to camp dogs and disemboweling several horses. Tracks were found. The culprit was a wolverine. A warrior named Buffalo Horn organized a hunting party and eight Flatheads—plus Shakespeare—set out to end the depredations.

Thanks to a light rain that day, they were able to track the wolverine to its den—a small cave. Thinking they had it trapped, they piled dead limbs in front of the cave and set the limbs alight to smoke the wolverine out. The wind was blowing just right and soon the cave filled with smoke, but their quarry did not come out.

Unbeknownst to them, the wolverine wasn't in the cave. It was watching their antics from the brush. When they headed for their village, it shadowed them. Their first inkling of peril came when the last warrior in line let out a screech. He had fallen a bit behind, and when they went to find him, he lay sprawled in a ring of scarlet, his throat horribly ravaged.

They decided to take the dead warrior to the Flathead burial grounds and rigged a travois. Since the tribe did not have horses back then, they took turns pulling the travois. They had not gone far when the man pulling it, who was behind the rest, screamed. He was sitting on the ground, his fingers splayed over his stomach, his intestines oozing out.

The warrior lived half an hour. He died stoically and bravely, his last words an appeal that his wife and children be cared for.

Two of them had died. They had debated rigging another travois but that meant two men had to pull, leaving them vulnerable to more attacks from their fearsome adversary. It was Shakespeare who recommended going back for more warriors and returning in force.

That was what they did. But when—forty warriors strong—they came to where the bodies had been, the bodies were not there. Both had been dragged off. They followed the trail of blood and found the first.

Shakespeare remembered it to this day. The wolverine had eaten the softer parts, the internal organs and groin, and chewed on the man's face. The second body was in even worse shape. An arm had been ripped off. A foot lay a dozen feet from the rest of the remains. And the wolverine had sucked out both eyeballs as if they were juicy olives.

They never caught the wolverine.

As was customary, the Flatheads moved their village shortly thereafter, and the depredations ceased.

Those two incidents, along with others, lent Shakespeare a respect bordering on awe for gluttons. Wolverines were nature's supreme predators, killing machines that lived to eat. They were not as big as grizzlies or as agile as mountain lions but they did not need to be. They possessed traits that set them apart and above their meat-devouring competitors.

Wolverines were absolutely fearless. Mountain lions might cower in fright when treed. Bears might bawl in fear when beset by hunters. But wolverines were *never* afraid. Cautious, yes. Endowed with that most basic of instincts, self-preservation, yes. But fear? An alien emotion.

Shakespeare had tried to figure out why that should be. Even grizzlies were afraid sometimes. Why not wolverines? What set them apart from all the other creatures in the animal kingdom? They were incredibly powerful and endowed with razor teeth and claws, but that alone could not account for their fearlessness, or bears and cougars would be equally fear free.

Wolverines were highly intelligent. But so were wolves and foxes and mountain lions.

Shakespeare finally came to the conclusion wolverines were so exceptional because of their exceptional force of will. When a wolverine set its mind to do something, nothing deterred it. Gluttons had the unique ability to focus their entire being on whatever they were doing at any given moment, with the result that random emotions, like fear, were completely blocked out.

Of course, it was pure speculation on Shakespeare's part. For all he knew, wolverines were so fearless and fierce because that was how they came into the world. They were simply being true to their natures.

And it was their nature that had him so worried.

Thus it was that on the third morning after the mother wolverine was slain and the morning after Shakespeare learned that Zach and Evelyn had found evidence of a glutton near the lake, that Shakespeare came out of the bedroom in his cabin with his mind made up.

Shakespeare did not want his wife to guess his intent. She would try to talk him out of it, or worse, bring her womanly wiles to bear, and he could do without the nagging, glares and pouts.

Blue Water Woman was busy cooking breakfast. They took turns. Shakespeare liked to cook and flattered himself that of the two of them, he was better—a belief he did not share with her to spare himself the aforementioned glares.

Now, grinning cheerfully, Shakespeare came up behind her, wrapped his arms around her waist and playfully nuzzled her neck. "Good morrow, fairest of the fair. How are you this most outstanding of days?"

Pausing in the act of taking a plate from a cupboard, Blue Water Woman twisted her neck and arched an eyebrow. "What's this?"

"I beg your pardon?" Shakespeare stepped back and put his hands on his hips. "Is that any way to respond to your husband's loving greeting? Verily, woman, thou art a trial."

"And verily, husband, thou art a windbag." Blue Water Woman placed the plate on the counter.

Shakespeare puffed up like a riled male grouse. "Now see? This is why women drive men mad. All I do is say good morning and you accuse me of having an ulterior motive." He could not resist quoting the Bard. "You are pictures out of doors, Bells in your parlours, wild cats in

45

your kitchens, Saints in your injuries, devils being offended, Players in your housewifery, and housewives in your beds."

"And, you, sir, are changing the subject." Blue Water Woman's English was excellent. She had decades of practice. She also knew her man as well as she knew herself. "What are you up to?"

"I refuse to stand here and be maligned," Shakespeare huffed, and stepping to the table, he took his seat. "Go to, woman. Throw your vile guesses in the devil's teeth, from whence you have them."

"Is that so?" Blue Water Woman absently ran a finger through her long hair, which was streaked with wisps of gray. Her lovely dark eyes were questioning. "Maybe I am wrong, then."

"Of course you are!" Shakespeare seized the advantage. "I am as innocent as a newborn. To accuse me of deceit is to accuse the sun and the moon of being blackguards."

"I like that comparison," Blue Water Woman said sweetly, "since your head is almost as big." She finished cooking and brought him a plate heaped with his favorite breakfast; flapjacks covered with a syrup she made herself from brown sugar and crushed berries.

"O curse of marriage! That we can call these delicate creatures ours," Shakespeare quoted.

Blue Water Woman set the plate in front of him. "If you choke I will not shed a tear." She handed him a fork and knife and walked back to the counter. "Are you going to tell me or go on pretending I am stupid?"

"You are many things but never that," Shakespeare said tenderly.

She filled his tin cup with steaming coffee and brought it over, along with the sugar bowl and a wooden spoon. Then she leaned back against the table with her arms folded across her chest and regarded him intently. "I saw how you reacted when Evelyn told you what happened yesterday."

Shakespeare stalled by slicing a piece of flapjack and forking it into his mouth. "Mmmmm," he said between chews. "Delicious."

"I know how you feel about wolverines. They are the only animal that makes you bite your nails."

"If that was your polite way of saying I'm yellow," Shakespeare said defensively, "then a pox on you and your insinuations."

"You are many things but never that," Blue Water Woman mimicked him. "Why are you behaving this way? Have we not always been honest with one another?"

Shakespeare sighed and set down his fork. "I won't be allowed to eat in peace until we hash this out, will I?"

"I care about you. I do not want anything to happen to you. I have become used to your quirks and would rather not spend the rest of my days alone."

"Someone has to scout around," Shakespeare said.

"Zach is younger and loves to hunt," Blue Water Woman noted, "and Nate does not have as much at stake as you do. Ask them to do it."

"They'll say I'm fretting over nothing. That I'm making a mountain out of an ant hill. But I've always been partial to better safe than gone under."

"Then ask one or both of them to go along," Blue Water Woman suggested. "I will not worry quite as much."

"They're busy. Nate has to finish Evelyn's bedroom and Zach mentioned something about Lou being so moody of late because he's been gone so much, he's decided to stay home for a few days."

"I do not want you to go alone," Blue Water Woman insisted. "I will come along to keep you company."

Shakespeare quickly said, "You will do no such thing. I can't watch my back and yours, both."

"Who asked you to? I can watch my own."

Smiling, Shakespeare reached over and patted her thigh, "It's really not necessary, heart of my heart. I am only going on a scout, not a hunt." He disliked lying to her. He could count the number of times he had done so over the course of their wonderfully happy years together on one hand and have fingers left over.

"You promise?"

"The truth appears so naked on my side, that any purblind eye may find it out," Shakespeare quoted with a lightheartedness he had to force.

"One of the things I have always liked most about you is that you have never lied to me. I will take you at your word."

Shakespeare wanted to kick himself.

"So we will consider the matter dropped," Blue Water Woman begrudged him, "but you must be back before the sun goes down." She lovingly kissed him on the cheek and went to bring her food over. "Promise me that you will or I am going with you whether you want me to or not."

"I promise." Shakespeare glumly poked at his flapjacks, his appetite gone. He would sooner chop off an arm or leg than deceive her. But *someone* had to make sure the wolverines did not pose a threat, and it might as well be him. He had the most experience. But he would not fool himself. The forest, the mountains, were a wolverine's natural element. He would be lucky if he made it back alive.

CHAPTER FIVE

Louisa King could not believe her ears. But then, she was dealing with one of *them*, and *they* could be the most pigheaded, stubborn, and unbelievably inconsiderate beings on God's green earth. Mad as a kicked cat, she glared at the brute she had taken as her husband and reminded him in her iciest tone, "You promised."

Zach King inwardly squirmed. When his wife got like this, nothing short of a miracle would change her mind, and it had been his experience miracles were mighty scarce. "But that wolverine could cause trouble. Someone has to go after it."

"Oh, no you don't," Louisa said. She was shorter than he was and a lot slighter of build, but when her dander was up she seemed to grow two or three feet. Her flashing blue eyes contrasted with her sandy hair. Today she wore a homespun dress, although she was not as partial to dresses as her in-laws. She would just as soon wear a buckskin shirt and pants. "You're not concocting some flimsy excuse to break your word to me, Zach King." She stepped up to him and poked him hard in the chest. "You swore that you would stay home with me for three whole days and I am holding you to it come hell or high water."

"But Lou," Zach said, marshaling his best smile. "The wolverine was spying on my sister. If I hadn't come along, it might have jumped her."

"Posh," Lou retorted. "It didn't attack either of you when you went into the woods." She shook her head. "You are staying put and that's final."

Zach felt himself grow hot with anger. He never liked being told what to do, even by his parents. He was notorious for his temper, but since he took up married life he had made great strides in keeping it under a tight rein. He reined it in now, and kept his voice level and polite. "You are making a mistake. I'm as good a tracker as my pa or Shakespeare. I will find the wolverine and kill it."

"Yes, you are a skilled tracker," Lou conceded, "but there's no telling how long it will take." Suddenly switching tactics, she placed her hands on his shoulders and looked deep into his eyes. "Don't you like being with me?"

Zach faced defeat. She had cleverly boxed him into a corner. That was the kind of question a man could answer only one way. "Of course I do—" he began, and she went for his throat like a ravenous she-wolf.

"Then enough of this wolverine business. You could be a week or more and I refuse to wait that long."

Zach clamped his mouth shut. What had ever prompted him to say he would stay home with her for several days?

Sensing victory, Lou smiled and kissed him on the chin. "I have been looking forward to this, Stalking Coyote." She only used his Shoshone name when she was particularly pleased with him, as a sort of special treat. "We'll go on a picnic today, and spend tomorrow fishing if you want. As for the third," she said huskily, rubbing against him, "we can spend that doing something else."

Zach wondered if they could spend it with him throwing her off a cliff, then was pricked by his conscience for the childish notion. "Whatever you want, Lou. I gave my word and I will stick by it."

She kissed him again. "Why don't you sit back down and finish your breakfast while I tend to our chickens?"

Resigned to an extended period of domestic bliss, Zach slumped in his chair and stared glumly at his oatmeal. There were times, he wryly reflected, when marriage was a lot like being in jail. He should know. He had been in an army stockade once.

Lou picked up a basket and moved merrily to the door. "We'll have great fun! Wait and see! I'll spoil you rotten even if you don't necessarily deserve it."

Zach rolled his eyes. Why did she go and say something like that? Women were genuine marvels. They could be silken-tongued and barb-tongued all in the same breath. But he could give as good as he got. He smiled and said, "Be careful the wolverine doesn't jump you."

About to work the latch, Lou glanced around sharply.

"You never can let something drop, can you?" And with that, she went out.

The harsh glare of the bright sun made Lou squint, but she barely noticed. She was thinking about men. Lordy, but they were exasperating! They could be as sweet as molasses one moment, grumps the next. If she lived to be a hundred she would never understand them.

Stopping, Lou indulged in a few deep breaths and cleared her mind. She refused to let him spoil things. He had promised, and they would have a good time whether he wanted to or not. She would make him.

Head high, Lou marched to the chicken coop. The chickens were a delight. She loved having fresh eggs every day. She was extremely grateful to her father-in-law for being so considerate. Nate had traded for eighteen chickens and three roosters and divided them evenly among the three families.

Zach had built the coop. It was a source of great pride to her that he had done as good a job as Nate and Shakespeare had on theirs. For all his faults, and Zach did not really have that many although she sometimes made it seem like he did, he was a good husband and a wonderful provider. Sure, he left her alone too often for her liking, but he had to hunt if they were to eat.

It was the other times, when he went off exploring, that peeved her. He would be gone for days at a stretch, leaving her to knit or visit with the others or twiddle her thumbs. She always managed to keep busy, and she was safe enough with her in-laws and the McNairs so close. But she did not like being alone. The nights, especially, were trials. She missed having him in her bed, missed his companionship.

So Zach could get as mad as he liked, but Lou was going to hold him to his word. She grinned as she bent and opened the coop door. Almost immediately the rooster poked his head out.

"Good morning, General Jackson." Lou had named it after the former president and military leader because it strutted around as if it were the boss of not just the hens but their whole homestead.

General Jackson came partway down the ramp, flapped his wings, and gave voice to a loud *cock-a-doodle-do*.

Grinning, Lou waited for the six clucking hens to file out, one after the other. The last was always Matilda, the smallest and the feistiest, and her favorite. All six were leghorns, the most popular of the laying breeds. Five of the six were white, but Matilda was buff. They laid white eggs, not brown like some. Each chicken weighed three to four pounds, compared to General Jackson, who weighed about six.

While they pecked at the feed Lou scattered about, she opened the side door and went in. She had to stoop. The roof was five feet high, the coop six feet from end to end. More than enough space for the nests and roosts. Today she found eight eggs but only took six. She and Zach were hoping some would hatch. Extra chickens meant extra eggs, and there was always the supper pot on special occasions.

Lou went back out, closed the side door and barred it. She was turning to go to the cabin when her gaze fell on a lone track clearly imprinted in the dirt. She had never seen one like it, and she knew all kinds after her years of living in the wild.

Puzzled, Lou hunkered. It wasn't a raccoon track.

Raccoon tracks resembled human hands, only with long toes instead of fingers. It wasn't a porcupine print either; porkies often came around late at night.

This new track was large. Five inches long and almost as wide. The outline of its pads and claw tips was remarkably clear. It reminded Lou a bit of a wolf track, but wolves had four toes and this print showed five. The rear pad was also differently shaped than a wolf's.

Lou sorted through her mental file of tracks and came up short. She was reaching out to touch it when the truth seared her like a red-hot brand. She knew what made it. The thing had sniffed around the chicken coop, just like its mother the other night at her in-laws'.

Fear knifed through her, but Lou smothered it. She had heard tales about the Skunk Bear. About how its kind were savagery incarnate, the ultimate killers. Rising, she walked quickly to the cabin and slowly circled it while examining the ground. Under the window she found what she dreaded: another print. Not as clear as the first but complete enough for her to tell what it was.

A damned wolverine had been skulking about.

Louisa bit her lip in indecision. She should let Zach know. She should also inform her father-in-law. But if she did, they might go after it, denying her the time alone with Zach that she had looked forward to ever since she talked him into it.

What to do? Lou paced back and forth. She refused to let the glutton spoil things. Zach would not go gallivanting off yet again. It could wait three days, maybe more. The glutton had not tried to kill their chickens or their horses. It had come and gone, that was all.

Lou speculated that maybe the stories told about Skunk Bears were exaggerated. Heaven knew, mountain men loved to tell tall tales. Her father-in-law and Shake-speare, in particular, took enormous delight from spinning colorful yarns. Many a night she had sat up listening to their escapades, wondering how much was true and how much was embellished.

Lou stopped pacing. She had made up her mind. She would not say anything. Not until after she enjoyed a few days with her husband. Then she would casually mention it, and if they wanted to go charging off to slay a bunch of hairy dragons, let them.

The week alone with Zach was what mattered.

Glancing at the door to be sure he had not come out, Lou swiped her foot across the print under the window, erasing it. She did the same with the track near the chicken coop. Satisfied, she carried the egg basket back inside and placed it on the counter. "General Jackson is in fine fettle this morning," she remarked, hearing the rooster crow.

"Is he?" Zach did not much care about the chickens. The eggs were nice to have, but their constant clucking annoyed him. As for the rooster, he had tried to pet it once and it had pecked him. One day he would repay the favor and have rooster for supper.

"Where would you like to go for our picnic?" Lou asked.

"I don't really care," Zach said, and winced the instant the words were out of his mouth. He made up for it by quickly saying, "Wherever you want is fine by me."

About to give him a piece of her mind about his attitude, Lou checked the tart reply on the tip of her tongue. Instead she said, "I'll bring venison and potatoes and the pie I baked yesterday, and we'll make a day of it up on that ridge I like. You know. The one with the great view of the valley."

"I can't wait," Zach fibbed. The prospect held as much appeal as a toothache. He might be able to induce her to cuddle, though, and he did so like to cuddle. But she rarely did it outdoors.

Not quite an hour later, they were underway.

Zach saddled their mounts, Lou packed the parfleches and he tied them on their saddles. They both were well armed with rifles, pistols and knives, and in his case, a tomahawk.

Lou beamed and gestured. "I'm so happy I could bust! Don't you just love our new valley?"

At last something Zach could agree on. "Yes," he admitted. Which was ironic, given that he had been against the move at first.

Their last cabin had been in a valley well to the north of his father's, and there had still been plenty of game. Zach had not felt any great need to move. But he liked the idea of being close to his parents and the McNairs, if only for Lou's sake. Now when he went off to explore new country, he need not worry as much. She would be well looked after.

As they rode toward the forest, Zach raised his gaze to the northwest. Far up on the highest mountain was a blue-green patch. It was a glacier, one of several his father said were scattered the length of the Rockies. Zach had not been up to it yet but he very much wanted to go.

A young Ute by the name of Niwot, who was courting Evelyn, had told Zach the glacier was considered bad medicine by Niwot's people. It was why the Utes shunned the valley and never set foot in it.

Since Niwot did not speak English and Zach did not speak Ute, they communicated in sign language. Skilled sign talkers could carry on conversations as fluidly as they would in their own tongues, and Zach was very skilled, indeed, but try as he might, he could not find out exactly why the glacier was taboo. The last time Niwot visited, Zach had brought it up again.

"Question. Why rock ice bad medicine?" Zach had to combine the signs for "rock" and "ice" because there was no sign for "glacier."

A stocky, handsome youth, Niwot had signed his answer slowly, choosing the signs with care. "Many winters past, nine Ute warriors visit rock ice. One come back. Friends all go under."

"Question. How they die?"

Niwot had thought long and hard, and frowned. "No sign." But he tried. He held his right hand close to his forehead, his fingers curled except for the first two, which were straight up. Then he moved his hand upward while twisting it from right to left.

It was the sign for "medicine," or "mysterious." Zach had responded with, "Question. How mysterious?"

Repeating the sign, Niwot slashed at the air with his fingers hooked like claws.

Zach had been at a loss. He went to his father but his father had never heard anything. Even Shakespeare, a living library of every story ever told about the mountains by red and white men alike, recalled only a vague legend that might or might not apply. Something about a *thing* that lived in ice and came out from time to time to slay every creature it found. It made no sense.

Abruptly, Zach realized Louisa had been talking to him.

"—no better time than the present, if you ask me. We're not getting any younger. Do you agree?"

"Of course," Zach said, wishing he knew what he was agreeing to. He shifted in his saddle and smiled at her to give the impression he had been listening. Suddenly a hint of movement seventy or eighty yards below snapped him fully alert. He thought he glimpsed a hairy form dart under cover. An animal of some kind, moving low to the ground. He waited for it to reappear but over a minute went by and the undergrowth was undisturbed.

"What are you looking at?" Louisa inquired, turning sideways to scour the lower slope.

Zach shrugged. "I guess it was nothing."

CHAPTER SIX

Shakespeare McNair headed south. That was the direction the mother wolverine had gone. It stood to reason, or at least he hoped it stood to reason, that her den was in that direction, and if it was, that was where he would find her young ones.

There was a trifling problem, however. "South" covered a lot of territory, square mile after square mile of rugged mountainous terrain, terrain that was heavily timbered and provided plenty of cover. Finding the wolverines would be akin to finding the proverbial needle in a haystack.

But Shakespeare had to do it. He refused to give up before he had really begun. He recognized the danger of allowing the wolverines to go on living, even if no one else did.

It was a grand day for a ride. The sun shone brightly, birds sang gaily, butterflies flitted among the flowers.

The feeling lasted until Shakespeare came to the forest. A preternatural gloom gripped the woodland. The trees were so high and so close together that they blocked much of the light, transforming the sunsplashed landscape into a pseudo nether realm. Only a few birds sang, and those that did sang timidly, as if afraid of being overheard by something that would silence their song forever.

Shakespeare rode with his Hawken in his right hand, the stock on his leg. His new white mare stayed alert, her ears pricked, which was a good sign. A new mount was always a bundle of unknown traits and temperament. But he had needed a new horse, and a settler at Bent's Fort offered him a good deal.

His old mare was in the corral attached to his cabin. She had given him years of near-flawless performance, always doing exactly as he wanted her to do without hesitation or fear.

Horses that balked or fought their riders could get their riders killed. The new mare had not been put to the test yet, but he was hopeful she would prove as nerve steady and reliable as her predecessor.

As Shakespeare climbed, the enormity of the challenge he had set for himself bore heavily on his shoulders. The wolverines could be anywhere. A single wolverine was bad enough. Two were twice the menace. Three or four were the equivalent of a horde of grizzlies.

Some might scoff and say Shakespeare was making more of their fierce dispositions than he should, but if there was one thing life had impressed on him during his decades in the mountains, it was to never, ever take danger, any danger, too lightly.

He was often asked how he managed to live so long when ninety percent of those who came to the Rockies were lucky to last five years. He always answered that each of his white hairs was a lesson learned, and that to stay alive a man had to always stay alert. And by always, he meant every second of every day of every week in every month of the year, a man had to stay as sharp mentally as his knife. Anything less, and he might as well dig his own grave.

Shakespeare tried to impart the lesson to Nate when they met, and ever since. It galled him that his "Horatio" *still* did not take some things seriously enough. The wolverines were an excellent example.

Nate should be with him, helping to exterminate the gluttons. Shakespeare understood Nate's new stance toward killing, though. There were times when he became mighty sick of it, himself.

The wilderness crawled with hostiles, cutthroats and hungry meat eaters, any one of which would take the life of the unwary without a moment's hesitation. Often the only way to deal with them was to end their lives.

Small wonder, Shakespeare mused, that those who lived east of the Mississippi River were fond of saying that anyone who ventured west of it took their life in their hands. Even so, Easterners did not know what they were missing.

Despite the varied perils, the mountains and the prairie were marvelous wonderlands of natural beauty. Peaks that towered to the clouds, capped by mantles of pristine snow. Cascading rivers and beautifully clear lakes. A wealth of timber: ranks of lodgepole firs, phalanxes of blue spruce, quivering aspens riotous with color in the fall, and more. A wealth of wildlife: gigantic grizzlies, shaggy buffalo, mountain sheep at dizzying heights, squawking ravens and noble eagles with their pinions spread wide, elk and deer and owls and chipmunks and all the rest. A great pulsing sea of life to be experienced and enjoyed, so long as the enjoyer remembered to watch out for the land sharks.

Noon found Shakespeare miles above the valley floor. He let the mare graze while he sat on a flat boulder and contemplated his long life, and the short span left to him. He was getting on in years. Over eighty, to be more or less precise, and while he was as healthy and as robust as a man half his age, eventually the years would catch up with him. They were already doing so in small ways. His joints ached on chilly mornings, and his body was sluggish until he had been up and about a while and downed half a dozen cups of coffee. Nor was he as spry as he used to be. There was a time he could go all day, like a steam engine, but nowadays the steam was harder to get up and harder to keep up once he did.

Chuckling, Shakespeare gazed skyward. "Quite the joker, aren't you?" he said aloud. "Stick us in these skin suits and send us out into the world with a smack on the fanny and your best wishes. We run the race, we overcome the obstacles, and when we get to the finish line, our reward is to fall apart and end our days as weak and helpless as when we came into it."

The mare had stopped grazing and was staring at him.

"What are you looking at?" Shakespeare demanded. "So what if I talk to myself? There's no one else to talk to out here. You sure can't hold up your end of a conversation." He laughed, and the mare went back to grazing.

Shakespeare could see the cabins from where he sat, so far below that they were the size of a child's play blocks. Blue Water Woman was probably having tea, as was her midday custom. He wished he were with her. He would much rather be down there, safe and doting over her and being doted over, than on a quest to bait fur-clad dragons in their lair.

"That's another gripe I have," Shakespeare said to the sky. "Why must everything be so complicated? Why couldn't you make it easier? We don't need the aggravation." He idly pulled at his beard. "Take these wolverines of yours. What purpose do they serve? If I were a cynic, I'd say you put them here, along with grizzlies and rattlesnakes and the like, just to keep us on our toes." The sky did not answer but Shakespeare went on anyway. "Why give life and promise death? Why is there only one way to be born but a thousand ways to die? Why wind us up and let us loose only to have us wear down and break?" He let out a sigh. "I don't mind admitting, between you and me, that you are a puzzlement sometimes, and a bafflement the rest. There is no rhyme or sense to giving a gift of fool's gold."

Shakespeare grew somber. "The Bard isn't the only one I've read, you know. I've been through Scripture end to end and back again. Eye for an eye. Love thy neighbor. Slay the Philistines. Him crucified. From one extreme to the other. But I've tried my best, and if I got it wrong, it wasn't from a lack of trying."

Sighing, Shakespeare stood and moved to the white mare. "Old William S. would be ashamed of me. I'm waxing maudlin in my dotage." He gripped the saddle and swung up. "What is a man, if his chief good and market of his time be but to sleep and feed? A beast, no more. Sure, he that made us with such large discourse, looking before and after, gave us not that capability and god-like reason to fust in us unus'd." He stopped quoting to cluck to the mare. "Now, whether it be bestial oblivion, or some craven scruple of thinking too precisely on the event—a thought which, quarter'd, hath but one part wisdom and ever three parts coward—I do not know why yet I live to say, 'This thing's to do.'"

The climb grew steeper. Shakespeare passed through shaded file after shaded file of leafy boughs and pines. The undergrowth was erratic; thick here, thin there, but always there were obstacles in the form of logs, boulders and talus. Treacherous talus; the ground might appear solid but it would shift like slippery grains of quicksand, threatening to pitch the mare onto her side and send them tumbling. He rode with the utmost care. He could ill afford to lose her. A man stranded afoot, as the mountain men were wont to quip, was a coon begging for an early grave.

Shakespeare amused himself by recollecting the tapestry of his life. His early years, when he did not know a mountain from a pimple but thought he knew everything. His years of exploration, when he roamed where no white man had ever roamed before, and in the roaming learned there was, indeed, much more to the world than he ever dreamed. His trapping years, when he plied frigid mountain streams and sold plews at the annual rendezvous. His middle years, when he lost one wife but found the true love he had assumed was lost to him forever.

And now? Shakespeare had seldom been so content. Blue Water Woman was everything he ever imagined the other half of his heart would be. He cherished her as he did life. He was happy, genuinely and truly and sincerely happy, a state as elusive as a ghost yet as precious as the finest gems from Samarkand.

He did not want it to end. He wanted to go on with her forever. The knowledge that it was not up to him, that the final curtain fell for all, made the nectar of their love that much sweeter.

The white mare gave a snort and pricked her ears.

Annoyed at himself, Shakespeare drew rein. Here he was indulging in whimsy when he should be focusing every iota of his being on his surroundings. He scanned the forest but saw no reason for the mare's unease.

"What is it, old girl?" Shakespeare asked, and fluttered his lips at his silliness. "But you're not my old girl, are you? You're my new girl and yet to be tempered." He nudged her on with his legs and bent to compensate for the angle of their climb.

The forest had gone silent, never a welcome sign. Shakespeare glanced right and left and twisted to look behind him. He kept one eye on the mare and saw her nostrils flare, but he would be damned if he could divine why.

"Leave it to the Almighty to give humans a nose as puny as their brain pans," Shakespeare grumbled. He would like to have the nose of a wolf, or a fox—or a wolverine. They could smell things a mile off.

A shelf broadened before him. To one side was talus. He veered wide, spotted a game trail and wound steadily higher through murk-mired firs. He realized he was scarcely breathing. "Valiant flea," he criticized himself. "I am not such an ass but I can keep my hand dry."

Above the firs was a belt of aspens. Shakespeare threaded through their pale boles, their leaves shaking with fits, courtesy of the northwest breeze. Here, it was sunnier and the brightness dispelled some of the darkling tendrils that clung to his confidence. "A pox on my nerves."

Another quarter of a mile brought him out of the aspens. Ahead, he beheld a welcome sight:a spring nestled at the foot of a bluff. He had a full water skin, but it was wise to use it sparingly and keep it in reserve for when water proved hard to find.

"What do you say, horse? Care to partake? Is this what you smelled?"

The mare quickened her steps and plunged her muzzle in the water. Shakespeare stayed in the saddle. It was too early to stop for the night and too soon for another rest. "Don't take forever."

To the west several buzzards appeared, soaring in wide loops in search of carrion. "Will you look there," Shakespeare grinned. "Rotten flesh is their delicacy. If anything has a gripe about their purpose in life, it's them."

The mare went on drinking.

"Don't overdo it, girl," Shakespeare cautioned. "Floundering is for fish, not horses." He winced at his pun, and raised the reins. "Let's go before you're so waterlogged, you'll have to ride me." He gigged her to the right to parallel the base of the bluff, but she took only a few steps when a loud, brittle rattling erupted almost from under her front hooves and a sinuous form slithered swiftly under a boulder.

The rattlesnake did not strike, but it did not need to. The harm had been done. Shakespeare felt the mare start to rise and cried out, "No, girl, no!" His old mare would not have panicked, but this one was young, and fear came readily to natures not buttressed by experience. She reared straight up, her front hooves churning.

Gravity would not be denied. In vain Shakespeare clutched at his saddle and her mane, but he could not keep from falling. He remembered to kick free of the stirrups, and a moment later hit hard on his back.

The mare nickered and bolted.

"Come back here!" Shakespeare fumed, pushing quickly to his feet. But he was molasses compared to the mare, and she was at the aspens before he had gone a dozen yards.

"Damnation!" Shakespeare drew up short and shook his fist in impotent indignation. He had not been thrown from a horse in years. It was downright humiliating.

Fear lent wings to the mare's hooves. Shakespeare stood and listened to the crack and crackle of undergrowth until it faded with distance.

Silence fell.

Complete, awful silence.

Shakespeare swallowed a desire to swear a mean streak. The horse was only being a horse. There was a chance, a very slim chance, she might come back once her fear subsided, although it was more likely she would keep going until she reached the valley floor, and the corral.

Blue Water Woman would be worried sick. No doubt she would rush to Nate and the two of them would backtrack Shakespeare's mare. The earliest they could reach him, though, was early tomorrow afternoon. Until then, he was on his own.

It could be worse, Shakespeare told himself. He had water close by, and he could hunt for food. His ammo pouch bulged with bullets and patches, and his powder horn was full. In his possibles bag he always carried a fire steel and flint and other items that would come in handy.

Shakespeare returned to the spring. High above, the sun was well on its westward arc. In a couple of hours, or thereabouts, it would set.

Something else would occur. Something that took on a whole new significance now that Shakespeare did not have a mount and a means to escape if he had to.

The wolverines would be abroad.

And they would be hungry.

CHAPTER SEVEN

The picnic was everything Louisa King hoped it would be. The site she chose was a sawtooth ridge about four miles from the lake, high on a densely timbered ridge. The crest was mostly grass with a few small pines. It afforded a marvelous view of their new valley from north to south.

Lou spread out the blanket she brought and placed the parfleches bulging with food and the water skin beside it. Humming softly, she arranged everything to her satisfaction.

Zach, meanwhile, walked in a wide circle, checking for recent sign of hostile men or hostile animals. There was none. He let the horses graze and did not bother to hobble them since they were close by. Plastering what he hoped was a happy smile on his face, he sank down cross-legged on the blanket, set his Hawken next to him, propped his elbows on his knees and rested his chin in his hand. "Nice day for our feed."

Lou smiled and nodded. "That it is," she heartily agreed. Nature provided a wealth of colors: the bright yellow of the sun, the distant deep blue of the lake and the far off green-blue of the glacier, the green of the forest and the white of a handful of large fluffy clouds drifting like airborne pillows. Nature also provided the chirping of sparrows and the sigh of the breeze to please the ear and calm the nerves.

Not that Lou was nervous. They were both well armed, and it was doubtful meat eaters were abroad that early. They had the day, and the ridge, to themselves, and she intended to make the most of it by enjoying their picnic fully. "I sure worked up an appetite on the ride here."

"So did I," Zach said. The food was always the best part of a picnic. The chatter that inevitably went with it was sometimes a trial in that women did love to prattle, but for her sake he would sit and listen to whatever silliness she came up with.

"I'm glad you agree with me," Lou said, while placing the bread on the blanket. "I was worried you wouldn't."

"I am always hungry," Zach said. "You know that." She liked to call him her "bottomless pit."

Lou glanced up. "I wasn't talking about the food, dearest. I was talking about what we discussed on the way up."

Zach remembered missing some of what she said, and wanted to beat his head against a tree. If he admitted his lapse she would be furious. She would accuse him of not really wanting to come, or some such female ridiculousness. Somehow he must find out what she had talked about without giving his inattention away. "Are you sure?" He fished for information, and congratulated himself on how clever he was being.

"Of course I'm sure," Lou said indignantly. "It's not a decision we should make lightly, is it?"

"Not many decisions are," Zach hedged. He waited for her to say more but when all she did was lay out more food, he tried again. "What made you decide?"

"I thought I covered all that," Lou said. She did not blame him for wanting to sound her out. It *was* a big decision, the biggest they could make, even bigger than the decision to move.

"Well, you know," Zach said, and shrugged, a tactic he had used before on similar occasions.

"We are not getting any younger," Lou recited the first on her list. "Granted, we have a lot of good years left, but why wait until we're so old we can't hold up our end?"

Although he was unclear what she was alluding to, Zach responded, "That makes sense. You always did have a good noggin on your shoulders."

"Why, thank you." Lou appreciated the compliment. "Then there's the fact our new cabin is bigger than our old one."

His confusion mounting, Zach sought to figure out how that applied to anything. "You always did say our old cabin was a bit small for your liking."

"Oh, don't get me wrong. I loved that cabin. It was special. Our very first home. You built it with your own hands."

"You helped," Zach offered.

"But you did most of the work. Remember when you

made the bed, and how we tested it to see if it would bear both our weight?"

Zach felt his ears grow warm. He was never comfortable discussing *that*, as much as he liked to do it. "That was your brainstorm." She was feisty in that regard. Not that he was complaining.

"Can I help it I adore you so much?" Lou grinned. She had finished placing the food out. Folding her legs in front of her, she wrapped her arms around her knees and regarded him lovingly. "Don't worry. We're making the right decision."

"I'm sure we are," Zach said, wishing he knew what in hell they had decided. Whenever she said not to worry about something, he invariably had cause to do so. "If you think so."

"Don't tell me you are having second thoughts?" Lou asked. She would be crushed if he changed his mind. "I talked it over with Winona and she agreed with me."

"You talked to my mother before you talked to me?" Zach's worry swelled. It had to be something really important.

Lou nodded. "I talked to Blue Water Woman, too. After all, they're both women, aren't they?"

Zach couldn't argue with that, but what in heaven's name being female had to do with whatever decision she had come to eluded him. Cleverly, he threw out another fishing line. "What did they say?"

"Your mother said she started even younger," Lou answered. "Not that they planned it. It just sort of happened." She winked and giggled.

"What age was she, exactly?"

Louisa laughed in delight. "Aren't you the kidder! As if you don't know. Not that we recollect much. But still."

Zach's temper flared. He resisted an urge to grab her by the shoulders and shout, *Tell me what in God's name you're talking about!* Instead, he inquired, "How much do you recollect?"

Again Lou laughed. She tended to forget that he had a wonderful sense of humor because he so rarely exercised it. "Not much. But who does? I have a cousin who swore she remembered her gums hurting when a tooth came in, but she always made all sorts of outlandish claims."

It had to do with teeth? Zach bought time to ponder by plucking a blade of grass and sticking the stem between his own. "I've always had healthy teeth. So do my ma and pa."

"They say things like that run in a family," Lou said. "There was an aunt of mine who had to have all her teeth out before she turned twenty. She wore dentures after that. When she married, her children were the same as her. Bad teeth."

Zach was glad they were finally talking about something he understood. "Bears need strong teeth so they can crack bones and stuff."

Lou blinked. "True. We're not bears, however, so cracking bones isn't all that important."

"Well, I just meant they have good teeth."

"I suppose most animals do. They would have to, wouldn't they? Or they wouldn't survive."

Zach hoped she would talk about something else. The conversation had gone from confusing to stupid.

"It's interesting, isn't it, all the traits things have? Bears with their hairy bodies. Turtles with their shells. Birds with their feathers and wings. Do you ever wonder how each creature knows to grow as it should? Why don't buffalo have wings? Or birds have horns?"

"Horns?" Zach repeated. Now it had gone from stupid to ridiculous. "Be serious. Buffalo can't fly, and birds have beaks. To each according to their nature." He had heard his father say that once.

"Sometimes you surprise me," Lou said. Levering forward on her knees, she kissed him.

Zach enfolded her in his arms and they sat admiring the view, Lou with her head on his chest.

"Days like this make me thankful to be alive." She touched his chin. "You are the sweetest man who ever lived."

"I am a warrior," Zach said. Before and beyond and above all else. He lived to count coup and one day be prominent in Shoshone councils.

"You are a husband first, a warrior second," Lou amended, "and before too long, you'll be a warrior third."

Zach did not see how that could be but he did not dispute her.

"I've never had a yearning to be more than a good wife and a good mother," Lou went on. "Hopefully, I will prove to be as fine as yours." Her own mother had died when she was too young to fully appreciate the nuances of womanhood.

"You will be," Zach predicted, to hold up his end. Truth was, he had no complaints. Lou did not cook quite as well or sew quite as well or clean quite as well as Winona, but she tried her best.

"Do you ever wonder what kind of father you will be?"

Zach had not given it much thought. He shrugged. "I will raise my son as my father raised me."

"What if we have a daughter?"

"I will leave her to you," Zach said, and chortled at the shocked expression he provoked.

"You will do no such thing! Daughters need fathers as much as mothers. My father taught me a lot." Lou recalled his death at the hands of hostiles, and felt her throat constrict. "He had his flaws. He was stubborn, and he always believed he was right. But he was still one of the kindest, most decent men who ever lived."

"That he was," Zach agreed, even though he never met the man. He pecked Lou on the ear and she smiled gratefully and snuggled against him.

"I wish he had lived. The two of you would get along like two peas in a pod," Lou remarked.

Zach wasn't so sure. A lot of whites looked down their nose at him for being half and half. To be fair, so did a lot of red men. Sometimes it seemed as if half-breeds were universally despised. And all due to a mischance of birth over which they had no control. Life just wasn't fair.

"Are you hungry? Would you like to eat?" Lou asked.

"The food can wait." Zach was famished but she was fond of moments like this, and he did not want to spoil it for her. He owed her that much. He wasn't always the most romantic of husbands, yet she put up with him.

For a long while they sat as they were, and then Zach kissed her and she melted in his arms, and later, much later, he squinted up at the sky and was surprised to find it was well past noon. His stomach rumbled, spurring him to comment, "We should eat if we want to make it back before dark."

"Oh, we have plenty of time," Lou said. She was not in any rush. Days like this were all too rare and were to be relished to their fullest. She lay on her side with her cheek nestled on his chest, supremely happy.

"Whatever you want," Zach dutifully replied. He ran his hand over her hair and closed his eyes, intending to rest a bit, but when a sound roused him and he opened them again, he was stunned to realize there were only a few hours of daylight left. Louisa was sound asleep. He shook her shoulder. "Sleepy head! Wake up! We've slept the day away."

"What?" Lou slowly sat up. Her mind was in a fog and she had to shake her head to clear it. "How late is it?" A glance answered her question, and she came up off the blanket in consternation. "It can't be! How could we sleep so long?"

"I'll pack everything up."

Zach started to rise but Lou placed her hands on his shoulders and pushed him back down. "Stay right where you are. We came up here to have a picnic and by the Almighty, that's exactly what we will have. We're not leaving until we eat."

Disposed to disagree, Zach swallowed his argument when his stomach rumbled loud enough for her to hear.

"See? You're famished." Lou moved to the food. "It won't take but a moment." She gave him generous portions of venison and potatoes, and handed him a fork and a knife. "Dig in."

Zach cut off an inch-thick slab of bread and covered it with butter. Nearly a third of the slice disappeared at his first bite. He chewed heartily while spearing a piece of deer meat.

"Want me to start a fire for coffee?" Lou never much

cared for it but the Kings, son and father, were addicted. A meal without it, Zach mentioned once, was like eggs without bacon or flapjacks without syrup.

"I can go without," Zach said. He raised the bread to his mouth and leaned back on his other hand. He happened to gaze along the ridge and stiffened.

The horses were gone!

In a heartbeat Zach was on his feet, the bread forgotten. Scooping up his Hawken, he ran to where he had left them and saw flattened grass leading south. They had strayed off while Lou and he slept. "Damn me for a fool! I don't have the brains God gave a turnip."

Lou hurried to his side. "They can't have gone far." She was confident they would find them quickly.

"We were asleep for hours." Zach broke into a jog. "Stay with the blanket and pray you are right."

Lou opened her mouth to object to being left alone but closed it without a protest. She should be safe enough. She was more than a fair shot, and her rifle could bring down everything from a wolf to a black bear. Grizzlies were a whole different matter, but her father-in-law had slain the only one for miles around.

Zach ran to the end of the ridge. He hoped he would spot the horses but they were nowhere in sight. They had drifted into a maze of firs. Half a mile down, a blue ribbon glistened: one of the many streams that fed the lake. It explained where the horses had gone.

"I should shoot both of them," Zach declared. But he was to blame. He swore bitterly and was about to turn and go back to Lou when from out of the shadowy firs came a strident whinny of pure terror.

The horses were being attacked.

CHAPTER EIGHT

Nate, Winona and Evelyn had just sat down to supper when there came an insistent pounding on their door. Winona was on the side of the table nearest it, and pushing back her chair, said, "I will see who it is." No sooner did she start to pull than the door was forcibly pushed open the rest of the way.

Blue Water Woman's normally tranquil features bore the stamp of deep worry. "Please forgive the intrusion," she said anxiously. "I am worried about my husband."

Winona had seldom seen her friend so distraught. Taking Blue Water Woman's hands, she pulled her inside. "What is it? Has he had an accident?"

Blue Water Woman looked over Winona's shoulder at Nate. "He went off to hunt the wolverines and has not come back."

"He did *what?*" Nate expected something like that

from Zach, but he credited McNair with more savvy. Rising, he came quickly around the table. "He went after them by his lonesome? Why, in God's name?"

Blue Water Woman frowned. "I tried to talk him out of it, but you know how stubborn he can be."

"All men are stubborn," Winona threw in. "They listen to their wives when it suits them."

Nate ignored the barb. "How long ago did he leave?"

"Early this morning. He promised to be back before sunset." Blue Water Woman gripped Winona's hand. "I am worried. Very worried."

Nate moved past them and out the doorway. The front of their cabin faced the forest, not the lake, a precaution in case of an attack by hostiles. A rosy strip as thin as a quill pen was all that remained of the day; the sun had set half an hour ago.

Nate's stomach muscles bunched into a knot. Shakespeare was stubborn, but he always kept his word. If he had promised Blue Water Woman he would be back by sunset, then that is exactly what he would do. He went back in.

"I have worn out the floorboards pacing," Blue Water Woman said in a quiet yet tense tone. "I wish he had let me go with him or taken you along but he insisted on doing it himself."

"He knows better," Nate said. McNair was the most experienced mountain man alive and never made mistakes. *Or was it a mistake?* Nate asked himself. From what Blue Water Woman told them, Shakespeare went off alone *deliberately*. Nate could only think of one reason his mentor would do that, a reason that chilled his blood and propelled his legs toward the corral. "I'm going after him. Pack a parfleche for me."

"Not so fast, husband," Winona said, emerging. "I am as concerned as you are, but you must not go rushing off."

Impatient to do just that, Nate stopped. "Why not?"

"Night is falling, and you can not track in the dark," Winona said. "Plus, you have no idea which way Shakespeare went, and our new valley is much larger than our old one. It would take weeks to search."

"I have to try. I can't stay here and do nothing."

Winona responded with her third, and most important, objection. "Alone? That would show the same poor judgment he did." She glanced at Blue Water Woman. "No insult intended."

"None taken," Blue Water Woman replied. "It was a damn stupid thing for that idiot to do." She said it harshly but she did not fool any of them.

"It is better to wait until morning," Winona said. "In the daylight we can track him. We will all go together, Zach and Lou included."

She made perfect sense, but Nate balked at the delay. "I should go on ahead by myself. Don't fret. I'll be fine." He took a few more steps but stopped when his name was called. Not by his wife, but by Blue Water Woman.

"Winona is right. It would not do to have you wandering around the mountains at night. Too many accidents can happen." Blue Water Woman paused and wrung her hands. "As much as it pierces my heart, we must wait until dawn to start out after him."

"But—" Nate said, and did not say more. Unlike him, they were not letting emotion rule their reason.

"It is for the best," Winona insisted. "The six of us can cover a lot more ground. And six rifles are better than one. We could easily drop a wolverine."

Nate knew better. Some animals were ferocious beyond belief. He had seen bears that were shot ten or more times, yet refused to go down. Mountain lions that absorbed half a dozen lead balls and tenaciously fought on. "Maybe just the three of us should go. We can leave Evelyn with Zach and Lou."

"You will not." Evelyn had come up behind the women unnoticed. "I am part of this family and I will do what the family does."

"Do not argue," Winona said. "You will be safe here."

"Don't baby me. I am not a little girl anymore, and I resent being treated like one." Evelyn added, "Yet you do it all the time."

"Zach and Lou are not going, either." Winona refused to give in. "Someone has to look after our cabins."

"They can, then. But I am going." When she was younger Evelyn always gave in to her parents' demands, but no longer.

"Not if I say you are not," Winona informed her.

"She can come," Nate said.

Startled by her mate's betrayal, Winona looked at him in puzzled appeal. "You side with her against me?"

"Evelyn has a point. We do treat her as if she is ten years old," Nate said. "When Zach was her age, we let him hunt by himself. It's only fair we treat her the same."

"But Stalking Coyote is our son," Winona said. Among her people, the males and females had distinct and different duties. The women set snares for rabbits and caught squirrels and the like, but hunting dangerous game was primarily a male pastime. So was going on the war path.

Nate was not one of those who regarded females as

inferior to men. Most were not as strong physically but they could do anything men could do, and sometimes do it better. "It would not be fair," he repeated. To forestall a drawn-out debate, he said, "I'll go tell Zach and Louisa. Give Blue Water Woman some coffee or tea. She can spend the night with us."

In ten minutes Nate was saddled and ready. He turned to the cabin to fetch his rifle, and there was Winona, holding it, along with his powder horn and ammo pouch.

"I thought you might want these."

"Thank you."

"It hurt, husband. To do what is fair is commendable. But life is not fair, and at times parents cannot be fair, either, for the good of their children."

"My mind is made up," Nate said.

"What about my mind? Is my opinion worthless?"

"Don't put words in my mouth." Nate hated it when she did that, and she had been doing it since he met her. All women did, according to Shakespeare, who claimed it was God's way of driving men insane.

"We are partners, are we not? Isn't that what you always say? We decide things together."

"Can't we talk about this another time?" Nate sought to avoid an argument. "I should be on my way."

"Go, then," Winona said stiffly. She would let the matter drop for now. But he had wronged her and there would be a reckoning.

Sliding the ammo pouch across one shoulder and his powder horn across the other, Nate accepted the Hawken, kissed her on the cheek and climbed on his bay. "Keep the door latched while I'm gone."

"Have I become stupid?"

Nate stared at her. Then he flicked the reins and rode north along the lake shore. A strong wind had picked up and the surface was choppy. His emotions were in the same state, as much from the hurt look on Winona's face as the blunder Shakespeare made.

It was always something. In the wilderness, every day was a challenge. Hardly a month went by that some new peril did not rear its unwanted head. At moments like this, he sometimes wondered if he made a mistake leaving New York City for the frontier. Then he would think of all the marvelous experiences he'd had and all the natural wonders he'd beheld and all the wild creatures he'd encountered and the tribes he'd met, and most of all, he would think of Winona and Zach and Lou, and know deep in his soul that forsaking civilization had been the best thing that ever happened to him.

Even so, Nate mused, he could do without the constant dangers. They wore a man down. It strained the nerves to always be alert, always be looking over one's shoulder and peering into shadows. Yet—and the thought jarred him—he had left the security of their old valley for the unknown risks of this new one.

"I'm a hypocrite," Nate said aloud. There was no other word for it. Or—and this thought jarred him, too—could it be that secretly he courted peril? Could it be that, like his son, he thrived on danger?

"Preposterous," Nate said, and fell silent. He talked to himself much too much of late. He must break himself of the habit.

Night had fallen. Nate rode in darkness, the forest to his left. From it came the screech of a jay and the faint crash of underbrush.

With a sudden start, Nate realized the window of his

son's cabin was not aglow. Ordinarily, they lit lamps as soon as the sun sank. He waited for the glow to appear but it did not, and when he could not take the suspense any longer, he brought the bay to a gallop.

"Zach! Lou!" Nate hollered when he came within earshot, but there was no answer. No one appeared. The window stayed dark.

He reined the bay to a stop in a spray of dust. Vaulting down, he took a long bound and stopped cold in his tracks. The door was ajar. "Zach? Louisa? Are you in there?" Again there was no answer.

Wary, leveling his Hawken, Nate moved to the threshold and gave the door a slight push with the muzzle. He went to enter, and his breath caught in his throat. Near the bottom of the door, clear and distinct, were long furrows in the wood; claw marks.

"Zach!" Nate kicked the door all the way open and sprang inside. The empty room mocked him.

The place was a shambles. The table and one of the chairs had been overturned, a cupboard had been opened and the pots and pans scattered about, flour covered the floor by the counter. One of Lou's curtains was ripped, and a small pillow she kept on the rocking chair had been torn to cottony pieces.

A musky odor was everywhere.

"Wolverine!" Nate exclaimed, and ran to the bedroom. The bed, miraculously, was untouched, the quilt tucked and smooth. Gnawing on his bottom lip, Nate scoured the front room for signs of fresh blood. There was none.

Encouraged, he hastened to the corral. Two of their mounts were missing. The rest were huddled together at the far end but had not been harmed. The most recent hoof prints pointed from the corral gate toward the mountains to the west.

Nate pondered the significance. Based on the bed and the lack of food odors, he figured Zach and Lou had been gone most of the day. The glutton had entered while they were gone, disported itself and left. But where had they gotten to and why weren't they home yet?

Going back in, Nate helped himself to a lantern and lit the wick. He carried it to the doorstep, and hunkered. Tracks showed where the wolverine had angled toward the forest. He raised the lantern aloft but the woods were too far off for its glow to reach.

Fear bubbled in Nate like hot water in a geyser; fear the wolverine had gone after his son and daughter-in-law. It was the only thing, to his way of thinking, that explained their absence.

Nate gazed to the south and the light of his own cabin. He had to go after Zach and Lou, and he should tell Winona. But they might be hurt. They might need him. Every minute he delayed might prove the difference between their living or dying.

"Damn!" Nate fumed, and raced to the bay. Mounting, he reined sharply to the west, and used his heels. Winona would understand. He hoped.

Riding at night was hazardous. A single misstep could result in a broken leg for the animal, and worse for the rider. On the open prairie it was not so bad, but in the mountains, with low limbs and logs and boulders, it was a fool's proposition.

Nate rode as rapidly as he dared. Since Zach had not mentioned anything about going up into the high country, they probably had not gone far. A mile fell behind him, and yet another. He neither saw nor heard any trace of them. In vain he scanned the slopes above for sign of a campfire.

On a wind-swept ridge Nate drew rein. Shifting, he gazed at the light in his cabin far below. He regretted not informing Winona. She would wonder what was taking him so long and head for Zach's place to find him.

With wolverines on the prowl. There were four, so far as he knew. They could be anywhere.

Torn between dread for his son and dread for his wife, Nate hesitated. Should he ride on or head back? He decided to go one more mile. If he did not come across Zach and Louisa by then, he would head back and wait until daylight. He had until dawn to make up his mind whether to go after them or after Shakespeare. It was not a decision he looked forward to making.

From the ridge he ascended a series of slopes, each steeper than the last. Most was thick with woodland. He was glad when he finally came to a clear slope. The sound of the bay's heavy hooves on rock echoed loudly in the stillness.

Wrestling with the decision he must make, Nate arched his back to relieve a cramp. The clatter of pebbles and stones was slow to register. Instantly, he reined the bay sharply to the left and heard it scramble for purchase. It whinnied as it legs started to slide out from under it.

Coiling, Nate jerked his moccasins from the stirrups and hurtled from the saddle to keep the horse from falling on him. A boulder leaped at his face. He twisted to avoid it but his temple struck hard.

A black darker than the night engulfed him. Nate was

dimly aware of rolling and sliding down the slope, dimly aware of dust in his nostrils and of skin on his hand being torn off.

Then Nate King was not aware of anything at all.

CHAPTER NINE

Shakespeare McNair had been in the woods at night countless times. When he sold beaver plews for a living, he often returned from checking his trap line well after the sun went down. Later, when he lived with the Flatheads, he spent many a night off hunting. Less frequently he joined in raids on enemy villages.

Shakespeare had never been afraid of the dark, so he never gave it much thought. The wilderness at night was the same as the wilderness during the day, only without sunlight. Different animals were abroad and different birds gave voice to different cries, but the forest itself was no different, and he always felt at home in the deep woods.

Yet on this particular night, Shakespeare could not dispel a persistent unease. He felt much like a mouse let loose in a barnyard to amuse a farmer's cats. To amuse himself, and take his mind off occasional stealthy rustling, Shakespeare quoted his namesake at random. "I will not excuse you," he chided himself. "You shall not be excused; excuses shall not be admitted; there is no excuse shall serve you; you shall not be excused."

In the recesses of the primeval mountains, an owl hooted.

"You boggle shrewdly," Shakespeare quoted. "Every feather suits you." Among his peers the owl was widely regarded as the wisest of the aerial denizens, a sentiment Shakespeare did not share. He liked to ask, "How wise can they be if they always ask the same question?"

Timber closed in about him on all sides, mostly pines with a smattering of deciduous trees. A carpet of needles cushioned his steps, and he made no more sound than a panther. As a precaution he stopped often to listen. His ears were not what they once were, but he could still hear the low cough of a cougar or the growl of a bear where others could not.

Stars blossomed. The moon was rising, but it would be a while before it shone in all its lunar glory.

The loud snap of a twig brought Shakespeare to a stop. He trained his rifle in the direction the snap came from, but after several minutes went by and he was not attacked, he continued down the mountain, muttering, "Foul whisperings are abroad. Unnatural deeds do breed unnatural troubles."

The trees thinned, and Shakespeare spied the distant light of a cabin. "So near, a raven could reach it in an hour, but so far, two-legged sloths like me take a day— or night, as the case might be."

Shakespeare was thirsty and hungry and tired, but mostly thirsty. He remembered the long drink he took from the spring before setting out, remembered the cool

GET
4 FREE BOOKS!

You can have the best Westerns delivered to your door for less than what you'd pay in a bookstore or online. Sign up for one of our book clubs today, and we'll send you **4 FREE* BOOKS**, worth $23.96, just for trying it out...with **no obligation to buy, ever!**

Authors include classic writers such as
LOUIS L'AMOUR, MAX BRAND, ZANE GREY
and more; PLUS new authors such as
COTTON SMITH, TIM CHAMPLIN, JOHNNY D. BOGGS
and others.

As a book club member you also receive the following special benefits:
- **30% OFF** all orders through our website & telecenter!
- **Exclusive access to** special discounts!
- **Convenient** home delivery **and 10 days to return any books you don't want to keep.**

There is no minimum number of books to buy,
and you may cancel membership at any time.
See back to sign up!

*Please include $2.00 for shipping and handling.

YES! ☐

Sign me up for the Leisure Western Book Club
and send my FOUR FREE BOOKS! If I choose to stay
in the club, I will pay only $14.00* each month,
a savings of $9.96!

NAME: _____

ADDRESS: _____

_____

TELEPHONE: _____

E-MAIL: _____

☐ **I WANT TO PAY BY CREDIT CARD.**

☐ VISA   ☐ MasterCard   ☐ DISCOVER

ACCOUNT #: _____

EXPIRATION DATE: _____

SIGNATURE: _____

Send this card along with $2.00 shipping & handling to:

**Leisure Western Book Club
20 Academy Street
Norwalk, CT 06850-4032**

Or fax (must include credit card information!) to: 610.995.9274.
You can also sign up online at www.dorchesterpub.com.

*Plus $2.00 for shipping. Offer open to residents of the U.S. and Canada only.
Canadian residents please call 1.800.481.9191 for pricing information.
If under 18, a parent or guardian must sign. Terms, prices and conditions subject to change. Subscription subject
to acceptance. Dorchester Publishing reserves the right to reject any order or cancel any subscription.

JOIN NOW!

sensation of the water on his throat. "Would that we could carry springs in our possibles bags," he remarked, and grinned. "I've lost my horse and any claim to be intelligent but not my sense of humor."

After that, Shakespeare became so absorbed in thought that he did not say anything. He dwelled on Blue Water Woman and fondly recollected the many happy times they shared. He also recalled their trials and disappointments, chief among them the fact they could not have children. Whether it was him or her they could not say, but something was not as it should be. All their parts worked, to put it delicately. Yet they had tried and hoped and tried some more until finally they admitted it was a forlorn cause.

Thank goodness for Nate. Shakespeare loved him as the son he never had, and adored Nate's kids as if they were his grandchildren. It tickled him no end that they called him Uncle Shakespeare.

Zach's fifth birthday came to mind. Shakespeare had brought the boy a toy rifle he'd carved from a maple limb. Zach had been delighted and ran around pointing it at everyone and everything and making a sound that was supposed to be a gunshot but sounded more like the squeak of a mouse.

Winona had gone over to Zach and bent down to tenderly ask, "Aren't you forgetting something, little one?" And when Zach looked at her in confusion, she whispered in his ear.

To Shakespeare's immense delight, the boy dashed over to him, threw both arms around his legs, and thanked him for the gift, exclaiming, "I love you, Uncle Shakespeare." Zach then ran off to shoot the stove, and Shakespeare excused himself to go outside. His eyes were misting and he had a lump in his throat. As he stood there composing himself, a hand fell on his shoulder.

"Thank you," Nate had said.

Misunderstanding, Shakespeare responded with, "It was nothing. Only took me a month to whittle."

"I meant thank you for the gift of your friendship."

It ranked as one of the two or three happiest moments of Shakespeare's life. Little did he know that by Zach's sixteenth year a change would come over the boy, and he never again said those words Shakespeare treasured.

Evelyn, on the other hand, said "I love you" all the time, but she was female, and females were generally mushier than males.

"Mushier?" Shakespeare now said aloud. "Is that even a word? If not, I should get credit for its invention." Chuckling, he switched the Hawken from the crook of his left arm to the crook of his right. In days of yore he could carry it all day and all night and not feel a twinge, but these days his arms cramped if he held it too long, and he had to switch back and forth.

"How ironic," Shakespeare observed, "that of all life's betrayals, our own body should betray us the worst."

Old age did not suit him. Shakespeare could do without the aches and pangs, without the cricks in his joints and the gout that flared when he overindulged in food and drink. He could do without getting tired so easily. Once, his stamina had been boundless, a vast roiling sea of energy that filled his every fiber. These days the sea was a creek, a small creek, at that, and he had to take a lot of naps or the creek dried up completely.

Shakespeare gazed at the multitude of sparkling stars.

"Whoever came up with this old-age business was a glutton for punishment."

At the mention of glutton, Shakespeare stiffened and scoured the woodland. He had not been paying attention as he should. Yet another sign of his advanced years.

The forest lay quiet under the firmament. Other than a doe he spooked and a bird that took startled wing, he saw no wildlife. He heard things, though, and his imagination always attached the same cause. But he had made it this far without being attacked, so his imagination, likely as not, was wrong.

Shakespeare's knees hurt. Of all his body parts, they betrayed him most often. Hardly a day went by that they did not remind him of his age, and hardly a day went by that he did not curse them for the foul fiends they were.

"Thou ruthless sea, thou quicksand of deceit, thou ragged fatal rocks," Shakespeare quoted, and sighed.

Almost simultaneously, a low grunt issued from out of the undergrowth to the south, not a stone's throw away.

Shakespeare stopped dead. A lot of animals grunted: grizzlies, black bears, elk, mountain buffalo, and the creature he hoped to avoid until he had a horse under him again. Whatever it was, it knew he was there, so keeping quiet was pointless. "Is that you, you great capering eater of carrion?" He launched into another quote. "A devil in an everlasting garment hath him, one whose hard heart is button'd up with steel; A fiend, a fairy, pitiless and rough; A wolf, nay, worse."

As if in answer, the thing growled.

"It is you, isn't it," Shakespeare said with certainty born of a musky odor that tingled his nose. He felt half relieved the confrontation had come. "Or one of you, looking for a meal."

The thing moved, a vague outline against the inky vegetation, a hint of size somewhere between that of a dog and a bear. But it did not attack. It growled again, long and low.

"Trading insults, are we?" Shakespeare asked, centering the Hawken. "Why, you're thrice a fool! I have the Bard for ammunition, and his insults are sharper than your claws." He didn't shoot. He might wound it and wounded meat eaters were doubly dangerous. He needed a clear shot.

As if it read his thoughts, the thing disappeared. It was there one heartbeat, gone the next.

"Come back and fight, you coward!" Shakespeare bellowed. He wanted it where he could see it.

The woods were completely silent.

Shakespeare was in a quandary. He couldn't stay where he was; the thing would sneak up on him and pounce when he wasn't looking. He couldn't go after it, either. In the heavy timber it had the advantage of sharper senses. That left one option. He lowered the Hawken, and ran.

It galled him. Shakespeare had never run from a fight in his life. But only a fool threw his life away and that was what it would amount to. He veered around a tree and had to jump over its fallen twin.

Fifty yards lower, Shakespeare came to a cluster of boulders. He raced in among them, ducked behind one of the largest, dropped onto his right knee and wedged the Hawken to his shoulder. When the wolverine came bounding after him, he would drop it in its tracks.

The wait was a test of nerves. Shakespeare figured the

beast to come on slowly, relying on its nose not to lose him, but when more than two minutes passed and it did not appear, he knew it was not going to.

Perplexed, Shakespeare waited another couple to be sure. Then he slowly unfurled. Could it be he was mistaken? he wondered. Had it been something else? A black bear, maybe? Had he jumped to the wrong conclusion?

Beyond the boulders was more forest. Shakespeare kept one eye fixed behind him, but he was not pursued. Whatever it had been, it was gone. Relief coursed through him, as well as annoyance at his antics. His imagination was playing tricks on him. He was seeing wolverines where there were none.

Shakespeare had no intention of mentioning it to Nate; Horatio would tease him. Nor would he tell Blue Water Woman. She had a tendency to overreact. She was also a master at making him feel incompetent, another of those female traits that made men want to scream.

Some of Shakespeare's unease evaporated. He reminded himself the valley was big as valleys went, more than seven miles in circumference, and that the wolverines roamed adjacent valleys as well. The odds of running into one were about the same as being struck by lightning.

The lit window in Nate's cabin was a sole beacon far below. Neither Zach's cabin, nor Shakespeare's showed any hint of habitation. Both were dark. That puzzled him, until he realized they all must be at Nate's. No doubt Blue Water Woman was enlisting their aid to hunt for him.

"That's my gal." Shakespeare chuckled. He could depend on her. In a crisis she always stayed calm. "But soft!" he playfully quoted. "What light through yonder window breaks? It is the east, and Juliet is the sun! Arise, fair sun, and kill the envious moon, who is already sick and pale with grief, that thou her maid art far more fair then she." He paused. "Of course, it would help if I could see her." That struck him as so funny he indulged in a belly laugh that died prematurely.

Out of the night came the crackle of dry brush, so loud that whatever made it had to be close.

Whirling, Shakespeare brought up the Hawken. He held his breath to steady his aim, but he had nothing to shoot. The woods had gone quiet again.

"Damned devious varmint," Shakespeare grumbled. He was tired of the cat and mouse game. "Are you related to my first wife?"

Nate would wonder why he was talking so much, but there was a method to Shakespeare's antics. The sound of the human voice was so alien to most animals that it spooked them. Although wolverines were as fearless as any creature that ever drew breath, he hoped his chatter would confuse the one shadowing him and gain him time to reach the valley floor where the open grass favored him and not his furry adversary.

Evidently it worked because Shakespeare was not attacked.

Soon he came to what he took to be the top of a slope. A gust of wind buffeted him as he went to descend. He glanced down, and saved his life. He had nearly stepped over the edge of a sheer bluff over a hundred feet high.

Shakespeare broke out in a cold sweat. Gingerly backing away, he turned to follow the rim. He could not say what prompted him to look back. But when he did, there it was, the dark eyes in the bearish head glittering demonically. A trick of the moonlight, yet Shakespeare could not suppress a shudder.

"Well, well, well," he said as casually as if he were talking to his wife or Nate. "You finally showed yourself, eh?"

The wolverine slunk nearer. Its rounded ears, its powerful body, its thick legs, its wide paws with their curved claws, its bared, glistening fangs; the predator was a living portrait of ferocity.

Shakespeare had the Hawken pointed at the ground. He slowly started to level it but stopped when the wolverine snarled and coiled. Freezing, Shakespeare braced himself, but the glutton did not spring. For the moment it was content to study him as he was studying it.

"You don't quite know what to make of me, do you?" Shakespeare began inching backward. "I must be ugly by your standards but you're no beauty by mine." He chuckled, provoking another snarl. The wolverine took a step toward him but stopped when he said, "You sure are a touchy cuss. Must be the stink. Is it hard to find a sweetheart when you smell almost as bad as a skunk?"

The wolverine let out a strange cry, half growl, half hiss.

"What was that for? Poking fun at me like I poke fun at you?" Shakespeare grinned, and was dumfounded when the wolverine's thin lips split in a sinister imitation. His amazement turned to shock when he heard an answering cry. Not from far away. From directly behind him.

Shakespeare half turned.

A second wolverine was crouched eight feet away.

The first one had kept him occupied while its sibling snuck up unnoticed. Now they had him boxed in on the bluff's brink.

Shakespeare uttered the understatement of his life. "This isn't good. This isn't good at all."

CHAPTER TEN

Zach King reacted instantly to the terrified whinny; he hurtled down the slope in long bounds and was in among the firs before the whinny died. He heard a cry from Louisa but he did not have time to stop and explain. He must save the horses if it was not already too late. Lou would be all right until he returned.

In the wilderness horses were invaluable. They enabled those who owned them to travel widely and rapidly, to reach water that much sooner and find game that much more easily.

The coming of the horse had completely changed the Indians. Tribes that owned them possessed a great advantage over tribes that did not, so it was not long after their advent that there was a mad scramble to own large herds. Horses were power, as demonstrated by the Blackfeet to the north and the Comanches to the south.

Zach had been taught to ride shortly after he learned to walk. Much of his life had been spent on horseback, and he regarded his horse as essential as his rifle and his knife. He would protect it—or in this instance, them—with his life if he had to.

Premature twilight shrouded the firs. The sun had not yet set, but the firs were so high and grew so close together that only random beams penetrated the gaps in the silent ranks. A cushion of pine needles was underfoot, but Zach was moving so fast he could not help making noise.

Another whinny drew Zach unerringly toward the source. He slowed to move silently and take whatever was after the horses by surprise. He was sure it must be a wolverine.

The firs abruptly thinned, and Zach came to a slope sprinkled with thickets and boulders. Below, its back to one of the boulders, was Lou's sorrel. His horse was nowhere to be seen.

The sorrel had its rump to a boulder and was flailing its front hooves at a pair of predators trying to get at its belly and bring it down.

Halting in surprise, Zach snapped his Hawken to his shoulder to take aim. The pair were wolves, not wolverines. He had seen wolf sign from time to time since arriving in the new valley but this was the first time he had set eyes on them. A male and female, they took turns darting in close and snapping at the sorrel's legs and stomach.

Zach felt a twinge of regret at having to kill them. He had a wolf as a pet once, when he was a boy. He'd raised it from a cub. For years they had been inseparable, until the wolf's nature would not be denied, and one day it went off to answer the call of the wild and never came back.

He fixed the sights on the male but the wolf did not stand still long enough for him to take a bead. It kept darting from side to side and in and out as it sought to cripple or disembowel the sorrel.

The terrified horse was tiring. If Zach could tell, so could the wolves, and they pressed their attack with renewed ferocity. He had to do something. The sorrel could not hold them off much longer.

Jerking a pistol, Zach pointed it at the ground and thumbed back the hammer. He did not try to hit the wolves since it was not a sure thing he would. That, and he was thinking of the wolf he raised.

At the blast, the pair whirled.

The tableau froze. The piercing eyes of the wolves seared Zach like lances. For a moment he thought they would attack. Then the male wheeled and loped to the south, and the female trailed after. Just before entering the trees, the male paused and looked back, and Zach, on an impulse prompted by fond recollections of yesteryear, raised his arm and smiled. Then they were gone.

The sorrel, meanwhile, was galloping to the east, toward the valley floor and the corral.

Zach gave chase but he stopped after only a short way. He could not hope to catch it. "Stupid animal," he muttered.

The crackle of brush warned Zach a new element had intruded. He turned, thinking there were more wolves, but the winsome figure that burst from the firs had two legs, not four, and the most beautiful eyes on the planet. Eyes alight with anger.

"What's gotten into you, running off on me like

that?" Lou demanded. "What in God's name were you thinking?" She had been astounded when he left her all alone. Husbands were not supposed to do things like that.

Zach pointed at the retreating form of her mount. "I wanted to spare you from sore feet."

"Are both horses gone?" Lou asked, looking around. "They are, aren't they? Wonderful! So much for my bright idea about a picnic."

"We'll collect the blanket and the food and head down." Zach handed the Hawken to her and commenced reloading the spent pistol as they climbed. He told her about the wolves. "I hope they don't make a habit out of trying to eat our stock. I would rather not kill them if I can help it."

"There are more than two," Lou reminded him, remembering the time they came across sign of a pack.

"They generally leave people alone, though," Zach said. But not always. Years ago, during a severe winter, a wolf pack had terrorized the Shoshones, and there were a few isolated instances of wolves clashing with solitary hunters and trappers.

"I can do without them," Lou said. She could do without anything that might eat her or her loved ones.

Zach gazed to the west. They did not have much daylight left. Ordinarily, the prospect of spending the night in the high country would appeal to him, but not now. Not like this. "Maybe we should wait to start back until morning," he proposed. "We'll build a fire and cuddle."

"Since when did you become so romantic?" Lou asked, grinning to lessen the sting. "You're not fooling anyone. I wasn't born yesterday."

"Thank goodness," Zach said. "I didn't bring any spare diapers."

Lou laughed and smacked his arm, then sobered as the consequences of being left afoot filled her with apprehension. She had lost her father to the wilderness. She did not care to lose her husband as well.

In addition to the blanket they had two parfleches. Zach slung one over his arm, Lou took the other, commenting, "We won't want for food. We have plenty left." Rather than carry the blanket, she folded it lengthwise and tied it around her waist, careful not to snag her pistols.

"At least we're going downhill," Lou said as they started off.

Zach grunted. He was preoccupied with the imminent setting of the sun. Once night fell, the meat eaters would emerge from their dens to hunt. "Stay close to me at all times."

"I am not a child."

"You are not Touch the Clouds, either," Zach said, referring to his mother's cousin, a veritable giant, and a warrior of renown among the Shoshones. Next to his father and Shakespeare, Zach admired Touch the Clouds the most of any man.

"I can take care of myself," Lou declared, a trifle resentful at being treated as if she were ten years old. He did that on occasion, and she always bristled. She was a grown woman and should be treated as such.

"I am sure you can," Zach sought to pacify her. The last thing he needed was for her to fall into one of her funks.

The sun slipped below the western ramparts and

night crawled out of its den to reclaim its dominion. The shadows steadily lengthened as the light steadily faded.

"We must stop soon," Zach said.

"If we walk all night we can be nearly home by dawn," Lou mentioned. In her estimation it was worth the fatigue.

Zach admired her grit, but he shook his head. With wolverines, wolves and God knew what else prowling the valley, they would be meat on the hoof, so to speak.

"Why not? Don't you think I can do it?"

Stopping so abruptly she bumped into him, Zach gently gripped her shoulder. "I know you can. But we have miles to go. Miles through the forest at night."

"So?" Lou persisted.

"Think," Zach said.

"I am, and do you know what occurs to me? You are coddling me again. You think I can't do it, that I will tire and give up."

"You always put thoughts in my head I do not have," Zach said.

"Then why? Are you worried we'll be attacked?" Lou patted her rifle. "We have these, and our pistols. We're crack shots. We can kill anything that comes at us."

Zach did not share her confidence, and said so.

"This is a switch," Lou complained. "Usually you are the one who shrugs off danger and I'm the voice of caution." She placed her hand on his. "Please. I don't want to stop. We won't get home until late tomorrow if we do."

Against his better judgment, Zach bent his steps toward the distant green bowl that promised sanctuary. He stuck to open ground as much as possible, but soon they were in dense timber. Soon, too, the shadows coalesced into the inky blanket of night. The stars and the moon did little to relieve the gloom.

Zach's nerve ends tingled. He kept expecting to hear a growl or the pad of stalking paws. One hour became two and two hours became three, and when the hours proved uneventful, he willed himself to relax. "I guess you were right."

Lou did not ask what about; she knew. "Of course I was," she grinned. "I'm female."

"And females are always right, even when they are wrong." Zach had not been married for so long for nothing.

"Two people can't help but have different notions about things," Lou said. "There has to be some give and take."

"Then how come the men do all the giving and the women do all the taking?" Zach teased.

"Says who?" Louisa rejoined. "Women have to put up with all your male shenanigans. It's no wonder God gave us the patience of saints."

"Says who?" Zach mimicked. "Females are born impatient and only get worse as they grow older. It's the men who have to abide all manner of silliness."

"For instance?"

"Women take forever to do themselves up. You nag us men to chew with our mouths shut and not leave our dirty clothes lying around and you throw a hissy fit if we track dirt in." Zach had a litany but she cut him off.

"You have just proved my point. If women put up with all that, and more, we surely have more patience in our little fingers than men have in their entire bodies." Lou smirked impishly.

"I have yet to see the day when a female—" Zach stopped and peered into the woods on their right.

"What is it?" Lou asked.

"I thought I heard something." Zach could not be sure. They had been talking too loudly.

Lou cocked her head. "I didn't." But she would be the first to admit her hearing was not as sharp as his.

Out of the northwest whisked a gust of wind that shook the trees. Zach did not move until the wind died and the trees were still, and he was convinced nothing was there. He trod lightly, alert for movement, but he might as well be at the bottom of a well, it was so dark. He realized with a start that if a wolverine or some other predator rushed them, they would be lucky to get off a shot.

Louisa sensed her husband was nervous and it made her nervous. He was not a worrier by nature, although he fretted over her constantly. More of that coddling she resented so much.

Zach would give anything for open space where they could make a stand if they had to, but the woods were endless. It did not help matters that the ground was strewn with twigs and branches, invisible in the night, which he could not avoid stepping on.

"At moments like this," Lou whispered, "I wish we lived somewhere nice and safe in the States." Not that she would ever go back. The mountains and the plains were in her blood. She had tasted the pure nectar of life as it was meant to be lived and she would not forsake it for the sham of civilized existence. In that regard she was a lot like her father-in-law, who valued his freedom above all else.

Lou was glad her in-laws were easy to get along with. Some wives were not as fortunate and spent their married lives miserable. She had feared the worst when she fell in love with Zach, feared his relatives on his mother's side of the family would despise her for being white, but to her considerable amazement they treated her as warmly as they treated other Shoshones. The color of her skin had not made a difference.

Lou was especially fond of Winona, who had proven to be everything she could hope for and then some: a fountain of love who worked tirelessly for the betterment of her family. Winona reminded Lou of her own mother, which was the highest compliment she could pay anyone.

"Listen," Zach suddenly said.

Stopping, Lou heard a sound she could not quite identify. It did not come from the nearby woods, but from far off. She turned to the northwest, racking her brain, and finally asked in exasperation, "What *is* that?"

Zach had no idea. It was not a roar or a growl or a moan or a shriek but somehow it was like all of them mixed together, a cry unlike any cry he ever heard. "Whatever it is, it's coming from near the glacier."

"It has to be a mountain lion," Lou guessed. Nothing else could make sounds remotely similar.

"Maybe," Zach said, although he would wager everything they owned that it wasn't a painter or any other animal they were familiar with. More than ever, he yearned to pay the glacier a visit.

The cry ended in a long mournful wail.

Lou could not repress a shiver. She was glad when Zach moved on. Still thinking about the eerie cry, she

David Thompson

nearly blundered into her husband when he abruptly stopped again. "What is it now?"

The answer came in the shape of a giant hairy *something* that reared out of the night.

CHAPTER ELEVEN

Nate King heard someone groan. He opened his eyes and winced in pain. His head ached abominably. Above him stars speckled the deep blue-black vault of sky. Rising on his elbows, he gazed about in confusion, trying to remember how he got there and why he hurt so much.

In a rush of vivid impressions, Nate remembered the talus and the fall. He reached up and touched his temple. He had a nasty gash caked with dried blood, which told him he had been unconscious quite a while. Judging by the position of the Big Dipper, it was past ten o'clock.

Winona would be worried sick.

Bracing his hands, Nate slowly stood. Immediately, his head began pounding to the beat of an invisible hammer. Clutching it, he closed his eyes and waited for the spasm to pass.

Nate supposed he should feel lucky to be alive, but he

felt more mad than anything, mad at himself for not being more careful. He scanned the slopes above and below for his horse, but the bay was gone.

In sudden concern, Nate groped at his waist. His Bowie knife, tomahawk and one pistol were still in place. His other pistol was missing. So was his rifle. Forgetting about the gash, he bent to search for them and had to bite off another groan at the torment it provoked.

The pistol lay an arm's length away. Nate examined it to ensure it was not damaged, then wedged it under his wide leather belt. He figured the rifle would be close by, too, but he roved in ever widening circles without finding it.

Nate recalled having the Hawken in his hand when he vaulted from the saddle. He had lost his hold on it when he struck the boulder.

A patch of grass seemed a likely spot to look, but it was not there.

Perplexed, Nate hunkered, opened his possibles bag, and took out his fire steel and flint. He pulled out handfuls of grass by the roots and made a large pile. Tree limbs would serve better, but he was fifty yards from the tree line.

It was the work of a minute to kindle a fire by puffing a tiny flame into existence and it gave birth to another. The grass burned quickly, casting a rosy glow some twenty feet. He stood up much too quickly and paid for his mistake with another terrible spasm.

His brainstorm bore fruit. Lower down the slope, metal gleamed. As the charred grass sputtered its dying gasp, he hurried to the spot. Smiling, he picked up the Hawken. But his elation was as short-lived as the fire.

The hammer was bent, and bent badly, either from being dropped, or more likely, from being trod on by the bay. He tried to thumb the hammer back but it only moved partway.

"Damn," Nate said, and pressed with all his might in an attempt to straighten it. The hammer barely budged. He had tools in the cabin to fix it, but that did him no good there on the mountain.

Resting the rifle across his shoulder, Nate started down. Of all his possessions, he valued the Hawken most. It was the one truly indispensable item he owned, the one that put food on the table and gave enemies their due. He was so accustomed to relying on it that to have it rendered useless was the worst sort of luck. But he was far from defenseless. He still had both pistols and his other weapons. Unfortunately, they were for use at close range.

Most nights the valley was alive with the cries and shrieks of its bestial denizens, but this night a strange quiet prevailed, broken only by the yip of a coyote and later, to the south, the wavering howl of wolves.

Movement registered from time to time, but whatever moved went elsewhere, leaving Nate to descend in peace. The pain in his head subsided to where it was bearable.

He hiked over a mile, and was passing through a tract of pines when the crackle of undergrowth alerted him to a nocturnal prowler. He figured it would give him a wide berth like the others had done, but it was soon apparent the thing was paralleling him.

Nate put his right hand on a flintlock, but he did not draw it. He refused to shoot unless the thing attacked. Several minutes went by, and he was about convinced the creature was harmless when a throaty growl proved otherwise. Since one growl tended to sound pretty much like another, he could not identify what it was.

To discourage it, Nate tried a tactic many in the buckskin fraternity swore by. He loudly declared, "Go bother someone else!"

There was a widespread belief among mountain men that the sound of the human voice was enough to discourage the most fearsome of beasts from attacking. To their way of thinking, the Almighty had given humankind dominion over the earth, and everything on it. Animals, therefore, were supposed to be subservient to humans. All a man had to do was look at an animal and raise his voice, and the animal would slink off in acknowledgment of its master.

It was not a belief Nate shared. Animals had minds of their own. Sure, some had timid natures and fled rather than fight, but for every four that ran, the fifth sometimes proved a fatal exception to the rule.

But Nate tried anyway. "I will let you be if you will let me be. What do you say?" he called out.

The creature could not possibly understand. What happened next had to be coincidence.

Nate was turning to go on when a hairy form exploded out of the forest. A snarl announced its intention. Nate drew his pistol and pulled back the hammer, but he was not fast enough.

The wolverine slammed into Nate like a fur-clad battering ram. The impact knocked him back. Teeth that could crush bone snapped at his arm. They missed his sleeve and his flesh, and closed around the flintlock. He wrenched to free it but the wolverine's jaws were a vise.

Growling viciously, the beast tore the pistol from Nate's grasp. A toss of its head, and the pistol went flying. Before Nate could recover, the wolverine was on him again, slashing and biting, and it was all he could do to evade its glistening fangs. He thrust the Hawken's stock at its skull, but the beast dodged.

Nate was a big man. Taller than most, broader of shoulder than most, more muscular than most. He towered over the wolverine like a redwood over a sapling. Yet for all his size, it was Nate who was hard-pressed, Nate who gave ground, Nate who desperately sought to save himself.

The wolverine was not the largest Nate ever saw, but it was large enough. It had a mouth full of razor teeth and paws rimmed with razor claws. Most of all, it had the spectacularly fierce nature for which wolverines were noted, a ferocity no other animal could match, not even Lord Grizzly. It had all that, and one element more; the wolverine was fearless.

Its glistening fangs missed Nate's leg by a whisker. He kicked at its face to drive it back even as his hand swooped to his tomahawk. But the kick put his leg within reach of its mouth, and teeth sank into his calf.

Nate had been bitten before, bitten by bears, bitten by a wolf, bitten by a mountain lion, bitten by snakes, bitten by a bat. But never had a bite sent such overwhelming ripples of pure agony coursing through him. He swore he felt the wolverine's teeth grate against bone.

Despite himself, Nate cried out. He tugged on the tomahawk and swung at the wolverine's head. By rights he should have cleaved its skull from top to bottom, but the wolverine's lightning reflexes came to its rescue. It bound aside with inches to spare, and the tomahawk's keen edge cut through empty air.

Nate thrust again with the Hawken, keeping the wolverine at bay. It skipped to the right. It skipped to the left. It leaped at his stomach, its forepaws poised to rake. Nate met it with the tomahawk, but once again the wolverine's incredible reflexes denied him a killing blow.

Nate feinted with the Hawken. The wolverine skipped agilely to the one side, and crouched. Nate paused, his tomahawk raised, waiting for his four-footed adversary to spring.

Neither moved, neither twitched. Every second was an eternity of suspense. A wet sensation spread down Nate's leg as his calf flared with a thousand prickly points of pain. He was bleeding, bleeding like a stuck buck, but he could not do anything about it until he disposed of the wolverine.

The glutton growled deep in its chest, its dark eyes glittering pools of pure bloodlust.

This close, Nate saw saliva trickle down its hairy chin. His own mouth had gone as dry as the desert. His palms, though, were slick with sweat, and he firmed his grip on the tomahawk.

Just like that, the wolverine sprang. Nate aimed a terrific swing at its neck, but a wave of dizziness caused the world to spin and his vision to blur. He missed, and the next moment the wolverine's teeth sank into his thigh.

Swinging wildly, Nate backpedaled. To his surprise he connected just as his sight cleared. He caught the glutton with the flat of the tomahawk, though, not the blade, and the glutton tumbled. Before he could exploit his advantage, the wolverine spun and vanished into the darkness.

Nate did not go after it. He was distressingly light-headed. From the exertion, he thought, until it dawned on him that the wet sensation had spread down his leg to his moccasin. He must be pouring blood. He wanted to examine his wounds, but he dared not take his eyes off the woods.

The night was quiet but Nate was not fooled. The wolverine was still there, watching him, biding its time until he made a mistake. But he would not give it the satisfaction. He would stand there until dawn if he had to.

Then Nate spotted the pistol the wolverine had torn from his grasp. It was only a few feet away. Sidling toward it, he braced for a charge that did not come. His foot bumped the pistol. He tucked at the knees, set down the Hawken, and without taking his eyes off the forest, felt about on the ground.

Without warning more dizziness assailed him. Dizziness so intense, so disorienting, Nate grew weak all over and began to pitch onto his face. At the last instant he recovered but it took every ounce of willpower he possessed, and he was left with lingering nausea.

Scooping up the pistol, Nate cocked it. He slid the tomahawk under his belt, reclaimed the Hawken, and used the rifle to support himself as he shuffled to a pine and stood with his back to the trunk so the wolverine could not get at him from the rear. Leaning the rifle against the bole, he carefully eased onto his backside.

The bites throbbed. His thigh was not bleeding badly, but his calf was, and his lower leg was soaked. Drawing his knife, he sliced the buckskin from his knees to his ankle. Blood bubbled from the calf wound in spurts. If he did not stanch the flow, the wolverine would be the least of his worries.

Placing the pistol in his lap, Nate cut a strip from the bottom of his shirt. He glanced repeatedly at the woods as he wrapped the strip around his leg. A broken branch served to complete the tourniquet. He tightened it until the blood stopped bubbling, then sank against the trunk, spent.

Nate fought an urge to close his eyes. Lord, he felt tired, as if he had not slept for a month. Palming the pistol, he gazed off through the trees and spied, far, far below, the light of his cabin window. How he yearned to be there! Memories of the warmth, the laughter, the love, were a tonic to his soul. He must not give up.

The throbbing worsened. Nate loosened the tourniquet, which helped a little, but he immediately had to tighten it again. The blood was beginning to clot, but it would be some time before he stopped bleeding.

It was unsettling, Nate mused, how quickly a man's fortunes changed. He had started the day whole and hearty and as happy as a person could be, and now here he was, afoot and weak and at the mercy of the merciless mistress known as the wilderness.

Something made a snuffing noise to his left. Twisting, Nate leveled both pistols. If the wolverine came at him, he would let it get close and blow its brains out. But the glutton did not appear.

Twice more Nate loosened the tourniquet. The bleeding finally stopped and some of his strength returned. Enough that he slid one of the pistols under his belt, struggled to his feet, and using the Hawken as a crutch, hobbled toward the cabins so very far below.

It was slow going. Nate could not put his full weight

on his hurt leg. Trees and boulders and other obstacles had to be skirted. Steep slopes were doubly difficult to negotiate. He was a tortoise, and tortoises were notorious for taking forever to get somewhere. He would be lucky to reach his cabin before the week was out.

Nate's leg began to stiffen. He flexed it to restore feeling, but the flexing did not help.

A hundred yards more brought Nate to a log. Turning his back to the trail, he sat down, grateful for the rest. His eyelids were leaden, and dizziness still plagued him.

Nate's chin drooped. He snapped his head up, but it was apparent that if he stayed there, he might pass out. To stay awake he thought about Winona; about how awkward his courtship had been, yet she fell in love with him anyway; about the births of Zach and Evelyn, forever enshrined in his memory; about the trials they endured; and especially about the happy times, more in number than the needles on the pines or the leaves on the aspens.

In his mind's eye, Nate saw Winona as she had been when first they met, so young and radiant, and as she was now, in the full bloom of maturity, still beautiful, still the other half of his heart in mortal guise.

Nate had always been romantic. His friends had teased him about it when he was young. His father had branded it childish, and done all in his power to stamp it out and mold Nate in his own cold image. Nate's mother was the opposite, as romantic a woman who ever lived. How sad that she had been trapped in a marriage where romance was regarded as wrong.

His mother's image seemed to float before him, a disembodied head in a black well of emptiness. She opened her mouth as if to speak but instead she pressed her lips to his leg and began gnawing at it as if his leg were meat and she was famished.

Nate wanted to ask her what she was doing, but his vocal cords would not work. Pain stabbed through him, and with it, the realization that he had fallen asleep. The image of his mother was not real. But the pain was, and so was the gnawing. Something was chewing on his flesh. Something was eating him alive. He tried to rouse from his stupor but could not.

Faintly, as if from the other end of a long tunnel, Nate heard a throaty growl of contentment.

The wolverine was enjoying its meal.

CHAPTER TWELVE

A wolverine in front of him. A wolverine behind him. On one side a sheer drop of over a hundred feet. Shakespeare McNair was in as dire a plight as he had ever been. To his left the woods beckoned, but he could not reach the trees before the wolverines reached him.

The pair were middling-sized as wolverines went. Even so, wolverines of *any* size were as savage as any bear or painter, and two of them made twice the peril.

The glutton in front of Shakespeare growled and went rigid. It was about to attack. Shakespeare dared not take his eyes off it to check on the one to his rear. His life hung in precarious balance, and if he ever wanted to hold Blue Water Woman in his arms again, he must be ready.

With astounding quickness, the wolverine in front of him sprang. Steely sinews propelled it at Shakespeare's throat, and Shakespeare instantly squeezed the Hawken's trigger. He was so close that he heard the *thwack* of the heavy lead ball. The impact twisted the wolverine half around in midair. It sprawled down heavily, head first, close to the edge, but unfortunately did not go over it.

Shakespeare swooped a hand to a pistol to finish the wolverine off, but he was not granted the opportunity. A tremendous blow to his back staggered him. He stumbled and nearly fell. Claws ripped into his shoulders and teeth tore at his hat and his hair. He whipped his body around, seeking to throw the second wolverine off, but it clung to his shoulders, its claws digging deep.

Frantic, Shakespeare twisted sharply from side to side. He reached back, gripped fur, and yanked, but the wolverine did not let go. Teeth sank into his upper arm, and he almost screamed from the pain. Dropping the Hawken, he swung both arms over his shoulders and succeeded in seizing the wolverine by the neck. More pain lanced his wrist. Ignoring it, he heaved, and suddenly the second wolverine was in front of him, savagely slashing at his chest and face.

Shakespeare flung the beast from him. The wolverine landed on all fours and came at him as he stabbed for a pistol. A swift bound saved his groin from the beast's slavering jaws. The wolverine did not give him a moment's respite. It came after him, snapping and biting, forcing him to retreat or be maimed.

Shakespeare aimed the pistol. His finger was curling around the trigger when he took another step back and his left foot met open space. He lost his balance. Pinwheeling his arms, he sought to recover his footing, but gravity had hold of him.

Without thinking, Shakespeare let go of the flintlock and flung both hands at the edge. He caught hold but came close to losing his purchase when his body slammed against the bluff. His shoulders protested with spikes of torment. Hanging by his fingers, he dangled high above jagged boulders.

Shakespeare held himself still, collecting his wits, his breath and his strength. His body pulsed with pain, and he could feel blood trickling down his back. He could not hang there forever. He must climb back up or he would tire and lose his grip, and that would be that.

Exercising the utmost care, Shakespeare probed the cliff face with his toes. He needed a foothold, but the surface was smooth stone. Gingerly, he inched first one leg and then the other wide to either side but found only a few slight indentations.

Shakespeare blinked sweat from his eyes and tried again. The fingers of his left hand began to slip. Freezing, he clamped his fingers so tight, the cliff edge bit into them. He slid his right foot along the cliff and back again. Nothing. He raised it a few inches and tried again. Still nothing. He bent his knee as if taking a step and moved his foot higher still, and wanted to whoop for joy when his toes dipped into a depression deep enough for half his foot. He immediately shifted most of his weight so his leg bore most of it.

Shakespeare smiled. He had bought himself some time. He bent his other knee and explored the other side but there were no holes or cracks or fissures. He must rely on the one leg, but it should suffice.

Girding himself, Shakespeare pushed upward. His right foot moved, and for a few harrowing seconds he thought it would slip out. But it did not, and he pushed high enough to see over the lip.

Both wolverines were on their feet. A dark stain matted the coat of the one Shakespeare had shot. As he looked on, the wounded animal limped toward the undergrowth. The other one had its back to him and was watching the first walk off.

Shakespeare pushed higher. The strain on his hands and his foot caused him to grit his teeth. His right leg trembled, and he worried it would give way. Then his chin cleared the rim and seconds later he had his left forearm braced on top. That was not enough, though, to lift his body the rest of the way. First he had to slide his right forearm up to join the left. He tensed his right leg for the final boost.

A low growl turned Shakespeare's blood to ice. He glanced up, straight into the feral eyes of the second wolverine. He had not heard it come over. They were nose to nose, its teeth bared to finish what it had started.

Shakespeare was completely at the animal's mercy. He could not defend himself, could not avoid its attack without letting go, and the moment he did that, he was a goner.

The wolverine sniffed his face, sniffed his shoulder, its fetid breath warm on his cheek and neck.

Sure his time had come, Shakespeare prepared to make the beast pay for his life with its own. He would grab it by the throat and the two of them would plummet into oblivion together.

Then there came a low whine from the woods from the wounded wolverine, and the glutton sniffing Shakespeare abruptly wheeled and bounded into the vegetation. Shakespeare could scarce credit his eyes. Thrusting upward with his right leg, he raised the top of his chest above the edge and threw himself forward. Flat on his stomach, he wriggled like a worm until only his feet were over the rim. Sheer joy filled him. He was alive! But for how long? Either or both wolverines might return at any second. He could not lie there.

The Hawken was where Shakespeare had dropped it. Scrambling over, he rose on his knees and grabbed his powder horn to reload. The crack of a twig changed his mind. He needed to put distance between him and the meat eaters. Rising, he lurched north along the rim but only for a short way. Then he veered into the forest.

For half a mile Shakespeare barreled through the brush like a bull through a cornfield. He made no effort at stealth. The wolverines would follow by scent anyway.

Fatigue set in. Leaning against a boulder, Shakespeare took stock. His back and sides were covered with claw marks and bites. He had lost blood but had no idea how much. His wrist was cut where the wolverine had slashed it, but fortunately for him the claws missed the large veins.

"I could be a lot worse off," Shakespeare said aloud. He had lost one of his flintlocks but he still had the other, and his rifle and knife. That reminded him. He methodically reloaded, slid the ramrod into its housing under the barrel, and patted the Hawken. So long as he had weapons he stood a fighting chance.

Shakespeare headed east. The wolverines were bound to come after him. The sooner he reached the valley floor, the better his odds of staying alive. Getting there was the problem. On foot he was a buckskin-clad turtle. The gluttons would overtake him before he was halfway there.

The minutes turned into an hour. The hour became two. Shakespeare saw neither fang nor hair of the carnivores. He entertained the hope, slim as it was, that they had lost interest in him.

"I'm getting optimistic in my old age," Shakespeare joked, and grinned. So long as his sense of humor was intact he could not be that bad off. "But I really must stop talking to myself."

Shakespeare tried not to think about his back. It had to be a mess. But Blue Water Woman would soon have him on the mend. Her knowledge of healing herbs was extraordinary.

The Flatheads, like most tribes, relied on a variety of treatments. Balsam fir was made into a tea for coughs and colds. So were sage leaves. Sandwort root cured inflamed eyes. The inner bark of the dogwood was good as a heart tonic. Juniper berries relieved bladder problems. Chokecherries relieved dysentery. Boiled elderberry roots soothed swollen muscles. And on and on.

Many whites scoffed at Indian treatments. Hokum, they called it, and refused to try Indian remedies. But Shakespeare had seen countless cures brought about by that hokum, cures that, in many instances, white medicine could not duplicate.

In fact, Shakespeare was of the opinion it was an old healer's medicine that accounted, in part, for his vigor and health. When he was a young man, he came down sick one day, his fever so high he was burning up alive. Otter Ear was sent for, one of the oldest and wisest men in the village. Shakespeare vaguely remembered the old man mixing crushed roots and leaves and flowers and bringing the concoction to a boil. The next he knew, Otter Ear was forcing the vile-tasting and even more vile-smelling brew down his throat. He had coughed and cursed and struggled, but the old man refused to stop.

The next day Shakespeare awoke to find the fever and sickness gone. Not only that, he was bursting with vigor. He had never felt so healthy his whole life, and he had been hearty and hale ever since. Was it his natural vitality? Or had the old man's potions imparted something special?

Shakespeare could not say. It was another of the many mysteries that made life so endlessly entertaining. He had never been one of those so soured on existence that they could not see the roses for the weeds. His cup always brimmed to overflowing, not half full.

Maybe that explained his vitality. For as long as Shakespeare could remember, he had a deep and abiding zest for life. Others were content to drift from day to day like driftwood on the ocean, but not him. He dived into each day as if it were a mountain lake, clear and cold and rich with promise.

Even now, battered and bruised and cut and torn as he was, Shakespeare did not give in to despair. He studied the terrain, reading it as intently as he read the Bard's plays, and when he came to a clearing bathed in starlight, he paused. On the other side stood a tall spruce that had been struck by lightning. The upper branches were a charred tangle denuded of needles by the bolt's blistering heat.

Shakespeare hurried across. Drawing his knife, he cut enough whangs from his sleeve to make a sling, and tied them together. He then tied one end to the Hawken's barrel and the other end to the stock. Slinging the rifle over his left shoulder, he gave a slight hop, gripped a low limb and climbed. It was rough on his hands and his back but he made it to the top without too much discomfort.

Up high, the wind whipped Shakespeare's hair and beard. He missed his beaver hat. He had worn it for more than ten years. God willing, he would find it again after he had dealt with the two nightmares.

Shakespeare rubbed a palm over a charred limb and held his hand in front of his face. His palm and the bottom of his fingers were black. Chuckling at his cleverness, he proceeded to blacken his face, his hair, his beard and both hands. He also applied black streaks to his buckskins. When he was finished, and settled in a fork amid the charred limbs, he appeared to be part of the tree.

The Hawken across his lap and his gaze glued to the clearing, Shakespeare waited. It might be minutes, it might be hours, but as surely as the sun rose and set, one or the other of the wolverines, or both, would come after him.

They were in for a surprise.

Shakespeare had not survived as long as he had by giving up when fate bore down. He was a scrapper, as his grandmother used to say. When someone or something tried to do him harm, he fought back as tenaciously as, well, a wolverine. It was part of the reason the French voyageurs had called him Carcajou.

Nor was he one of those who believed a person's destiny was etched in stone. The notion that everything a person did from cradle to grave was foreordained was absurd. To disprove it, all someone had to do was hold out both hands and pick one.

Shakespeare believed that everyone molded their own lives, that the decisions made today determined every tomorrow. Whether he lived to see the next dawn or whether the wolverines feasted on his flesh was not in the hands of fickle fate. It was in his hands. He would have no one to blame but himself if he lost their benighted game of life and death.

Midnight came and went. Shakespeare did not move, did not stretch, did not cough. He did not do anything to give his presence away. His mind moved, though. Shakespeare traveled back to his first meeting with Nate, a youth so green, elk mistook him for grass. He had seen Nate grow from a stripling into manhood, and been as proud of the younger man's accomplishments as if they were those of his own son.

Shakespeare's keenest regret was that he never had children, a son or a daughter he could pamper, and to whom he could impart the kernels of wisdom gleaned during a long and eventful life. Thankfully, Nate King had come along to fill the emptiness in his heart and prove that if a person wanted something deeply enough and dearly enough, their dreams came true.

With a start, Shakespeare jerked his head up. He had started to doze off. Another minute and he would saw charred logs.

Upset with himself, Shakespeare gazed at the clearing—and felt his breath catch in his throat.

A squat form had emerged from the undergrowth. Nose held high, it was testing the wind.

Shakespeare's mouth quirked upward. His ploy had worked. The wolverine was about to blunder into his gun sights. He slowly tucked the stock to his shoulder and began elevating the barrel. He would wait until the glutton was closer so as not to miss.

A second form appeared. It limped up to the first and they touched noses. Together they started across the clearing.

Another couple of inches and Shakespeare would have the Hawken level. He pressed his cheek to the stock. Suddenly the tip of the muzzle grazed a branch. There was the slightest of sounds, a *scrtich* that Shakespeare barely heard. Yet the keen ears of the gluttons heard it, too. They stopped cold in their tracks. In unison, their heads swung up. In unison, they sniffed and fixed their glittering eyes on the charred limbs. In unison, they growled.

They knew he was there.

CHAPTER THIRTEEN

Zach King was rash and headstrong and possessed more than common courage, but he was not a fool. Had he been alone when the giant creature reared out of the night, he would have whirled and bolted to the nearest tree and clambered out of reach with the agility of a squirrel. But he was not alone. His wife was with him, frozen in shock. She could not reach a tree before the thing reached them.

Some men might have tried to save themselves, but not Zach. He would never desert Louisa. She was his heart made flesh, his soul in corporal form. He loved her clear down to the marrow in his bones, and would gladly give his own life, if need be, to preserve hers.

So now Zach jerked his rifle to his shoulder, saying, "When it attacks, I'll hold it off and you run!"

"Nothing doing," Louisa said, and stepped up beside

him so they were shoulder to shoulder, her own rifle rising.

Zach never loved her more than at that moment, although he wanted to grip her by the arms and shake her until her teeth rattled for not heeding him. But then, she always did have a mind of her own.

The creature, though, had not attacked. It snorted and took a lumbering step nearer, enabling them to recognize it.

Zach's blood raced faster in his veins. When he first saw it, he took it to be a bear, an illusion fostered by the darkness and the fact he was facing it head-on. But now he could see its horns and forelegs.

Few who lived east of the Mississippi River realized there were two types of buffalo. Most thought of the giant brutes of the plains, wandering in countless millions over the unspoiled prairie. But there were other buffalo. Buffalo that preferred the mountains to the plains. The mountain men, quite naturally, called them mountain buffalo, and in many respects they were much like their lowland counterparts. They grew as big, with the males six feet high at the shoulder and over twelve feet long. They were generally dark brown, and had long tails with tufts at the end. Both the bulls and the cows had horns, wicked black curved scimitars with a spread of three feet or more. The main differences were that mountain buffalo were shaggier, and their dispositions were much more excitable. They usually fled at the sight of man, but when cornered or taken by surprise, they had been known to gore and trample an unwary rider.

Zach felt sure the buffalo would charge. They were so close, he saw stars gleam in its eyes. So close, the wheeze of its heavy breaths was like the wheeze of a blacksmith's bellows.

The buffalo snorted and pawed the ground and shook its great massive head with those terrible twin horns.

"Do we shoot it or not?" Lou whispered. She trusted his judgment. He knew all there was to know about wild animals, thanks to seasoned veterans like his father and Shakespeare McNair, and his own lifelong experiences.

The buffalo raised its head and stared fixedly at Louisa. Its nostrils widened in a loud sniff.

Suddenly the huge head dipped, prelude to an attack. Zach instantly stepped between the beast and his wife and fixed a bead on the creature's right eye. The skull was too thick for a lead ball to penetrate.

Lou almost shoved him aside. She would not let him sell his life to save hers. If they died, they died together, as befitted two people who had become one in their heart of hearts.

But then the buffalo snorted again, wheeled, and went off through the vegetation with the speed and stealth of a runaway wagon. The crash and crackling went on for a long time, finally fading to silence.

Zach let out the breath he had not realized he was holding. Lowering his Hawken, he grinned crookedly. "We were lucky."

"Your father said there was a small herd of them up here," Lou mentioned. "Fifteen or twenty, I believe."

"There will be one less before the month is out," Zach predicted. "I have a hankering for buffalo meat."

"Let's keep going." The incident had heightened Lou's sense of unease. She never much liked the woods at night, especially the primordial forest of the Rockies. Here the hands of time had stopped. The mile-high mountains and the vast untamed forests that covered them were much like creation at the dawn of all things, when people were few and the wild things reigned.

Zach was extra vigilant from then on. He blamed himself for not spotting the buffalo sooner; his lapses could get Lou killed.

The dense timber was oppressive, rank after rank of pine and fir sentinels choked by undergrowth. In daylight navigating the terrain was difficult enough, at night it was a nightmare. The press of vegetation, the ominous silence broken by eerie cries and shrieks, and the inky blackness conspired to fill them with foreboding.

Zach tried to shrug it off. Neither the wolves nor the buffalo had attacked them, and odds were, anything else they encountered wouldn't either. Most animals avoided humans.

Ironically, the most dangerous denizen of the wilds was other humans, and fortunately, the only inhabitants of the valley were his family and the McNairs. No tribe claimed it as part of the tribe's territory, which was strange. No other white men ever passed through because it was so far into the mountains and so far from any established trails. It was theirs and theirs alone, and Zach would not have it any other way.

So there was really no reason for Zach to worry. But he did. He could not shake the persistent feeling that they were *not* alone, that something had been shadowing them since before they lost their horses.

"It's spooky out here at night, isn't it?" Lou said. She would rather talk than have the silence.

"Not really," Zach said, to put her at ease.

"You don't think so? I do, and I'm not ashamed to admit it."

Zach did think so, but men did not let on if they were spooked. "I have never been scared of the dark."

Out of the blue, Louisa asked, "When will you start on the new room? There's plenty of time, but we shouldn't wait until the last minute."

"What new room?" Zach glanced at her in confusion. Their cabin was done. They had never talked about adding on. He suspected it must have something to do with whatever she said earlier when he was not listening. Her next words proved his hunch right.

"After our talk, we will need one," Louisa said. "Not a big one, but big enough."

Big enough for what? Zach asked himself. He was afraid to ask the question out loud.

"I'd say one as big as Evelyn's will do us," Lou continued. "I'll decorate it myself, if you don't mind."

"Why would I?" Zach could afford to be gracious when he had no idea in hell what she was talking about.

"Although, now that I think about it, I can't pick fabric because we won't know in advance, but if I don't choose, then there won't be any curtains and whatnot." Louisa paused. "What do you think?"

Zach wished they would stumble on another buffalo. Anything to distract her. "I think that whatever you think is fine by me."

"You can be so sweet sometimes."

Congratulating himself on his narrow escape, Zach grinned and skirted a log. A blur of motion low to the ground registered on the periphery of his vision. Teeth sheared into his right leg. Involuntary, he cried out as his leg was violently yanked out from under him and he pitched onto his belly.

That was when Lou screamed.

Winona King straightened and announced, "I have waited long enough. Something is dreadfully wrong. I am going after them."

"At this time of night?" Blue Water Woman shook her head. "What good would it do? It is better to wait until morning."

Evelyn wholeheartedly agreed. The thought of her mother wandering the woods at night petrified her. "It's too dangerous."

To Winona, the perils counted for little when weighed against the lives of her husband and her oldest. After Nate failed to come back from Zach's, she had ridden over to her son's cabin just before sunset. The tracks, the shambles, the hoofprints of Nate's mount, all the pieces solved the puzzle of his absence.

Winona had boiled with anger. She rarely lost her temper, but it was outright foolish of Nate—and inconsiderate—to venture up into the high country without telling her. She came home to await his return, but as the hours crawled by and her man did not show up, her anger gave way to gnawing anxiety.

Winona hid it well. She had been trained at an early age not to betray her emotions. Shoshone children were expected to behave calmly in a crisis. Screaming, crying, hysterics were frowned on.

Once, Winona had been playing with her doll near the family's lodge. Shouts had erupted, along with fierce war whoops and loud whinnies. She had looked up, mystified by the uproar, and her mother dashed up, scooped Winona into her arms and ran to the flap. As her mother ducked to carry her inside, Winona glimpsed other mothers and children running to their lodges. She saw warriors race toward the horse herd, some nocking arrows to bow strings, others armed with lances, a few with rifles. It dawned on her that their village was being raided. Her mother had warned her it might happen someday, and that when it did, she was to hide under a buffalo robe until her mother said it was safe to come out.

Winona remembered it being hot and stuffy under that robe. As her mother was pushing her under, her father rushed into the lodge after his bow. "The Blackfeet!" he had shouted, and he and her mother ran back out.

Panic gripped Winona. They had left her alone. She clutched the doll to her so tightly, her fingers hurt. Outside, bedlam reigned. Yells and shrieks and whoops fell on her tender ears in riotous cacophony.

Suddenly the flap opened again, and in darted a strange warrior. One peek, and Winona knew he was not a Shoshone. His hair was different, and he was painted for war. To her, he was the most terrifying thing she ever saw.

The warrior glanced quickly about the lodge. He turned and was about to go back out when his gaze fell on the buffalo robe.

Winona realized she had been shaking with fear. She willed herself to stop, but it was too late.

The Blackfoot had whipped the robe off the ground. Winona recoiled and opened her mouth to scream, then promptly closed it again. Her mother had told her she must not make any noise and that was exactly what she would do.

The warrior cast the robe aside. Grabbing her arm, he jerked her to her feet and peered hard at her face. He raised his other hand, and the lance it held, aloft.

Winona had returned his scrutiny calmly. Inwardly she was terrified, but outwardly she had regarded him with interest. His nose was big and hooked like a bird's beak. His eyes were so close together, he almost looked cross-eyed. She thought it funny, and grinned.

The warrior gave a little start, then did the last thing she expected; he grinned back. Gently, he removed his hand and said something in his tongue. Then he patted her head, and left.

Winona immediately crawled back under the robe. She stayed there for what seemed forever, listening to cries of war and pain. At last her mother came, and carried her outside.

The Blackfeet had been repulsed, but not without loss. Two Shoshones had been slain, fourteen horses stolen. Coup had been counted on the enemy, and several dead Blackfeet were laid out in a row.

Winona's mother had taken her to see them. She distinctly recalled gazing down at them from the safety of her mother's arms and hoping the warrior who spared her was not one of them. He wasn't, and Winona had giggled in relief.

"Death is not to be laughed at, daughter." Her mother had misunderstood. "Always show respect, even for an enemy."

Just one of the many important lessons Winona

learned at an early age. Now, with her daughter and her best friend giving her stern looks of disapproval, she said, "They might need help. I cannot just sit here."

"Do you think it is easier on us?" Blue Water Woman countered.

Evelyn had a better argument. "Aren't you the one who always tells Zach not to go rushing off half-cocked? Aren't you the one who always says we must keep our wits about us?"

"I am not your brother," Winona said indignantly.

"You are acting like him." Evelyn refused to be cowed. "He always does things without thinking them through."

A comment about daughters who did not show proper respect for their elders was on the tip of Winona's tongue, but she bit it off. They were right and she was wrong. She had taken her son to task many times for behaving exactly as she was behaving. "Very well."

Evelyn was still talking and did not hear her. "Don't let our feelings get us killed. Isn't that what you have told us time and again? Like when Zach helped wipe out those traders who were trying to start a war between the Shoshones and the Crows? Or when Zach took it on himself to pay the Piegans a visit after they killed a Shoshone friend of his?" Evelyn blinked. "What did you just say?"

"I will wait until first light, then go."

"No," Blue Water Woman amended, "*we* will wait until first light and go together. Or have you forgotten my husband is missing as well?"

Winona held out her hands and they came to her and

each clasped one. "The three of us will go," she agreed. She was not leaving Evelyn alone with wolverines on the rampage. "Now get some sleep. We will need it."

Squealing in delight, Evelyn kissed her mother on the cheek. The next moment, though, her bubble burst.

"You will do exactly as I say at all times, daughter. If you do not, you might not make it back alive."

Chapter Fourteen

Nate King's eyes snapped open. "No!" he cried and pushed to his feet. He swung his pistol from side to side, seeking a target. But there was none. The wolverine was not there. It had not been devouring him. The whole thing had been a figment of his mind.

Cold sweat caked Nate from hair to toe. More dizziness assailed him, and his leg throbbed worse than ever. He loosened the tourniquet briefly, but that did not help. Determined not to fall asleep again, he braced the Hawken under his arm and limped on down the mountain.

Nate's main worry was infection. Animal attacks were not always fatal, but the infections that resulted from them invariably were. Animals never cleaned their teeth, never gargled. Their mouths became rank with foul odors from all the blood and juicy fat and gore, to say nothing of those that ate carrion. Bits of putrid meat lodged between their teeth and rotted there.

One bite, one nip, was sometimes enough to bring on a raging fever and a slow, agonizing death. Doctors did what they could but once infection set in, surviving was an uphill struggle.

Out here in the wilderness, with no doctor or healer to tend him, Nate would not last long. He must get to the cabin, get to Winona and Blue Water Woman. They knew remedies that would have him spry and hale in a week or two.

Nate wiped his sleeve across his brow, but new beads of sweat formed almost before he lowered his arm. He grew cold inside, as cold as the ancient glacier high on the northwest peak, and he could not stop bouts of intense shivering. Soon he grew hot, so hot he wanted to tear off his buckskins for relief. His skin burned like the surface of the sun, and the sweat worsened until it dripped from his chin like drops of rain.

The trees thinned. Far below, the glow in his cabin window drew Nate on. He did not take his eyes off it. An ache formed in his chest, an ache that had nothing to do with his injuries. His throat became constricted and he swallowed several times to relieve the knot.

"Winona," Nate said softly. It came out more as the croak of a frog than a tender term of endearment.

The night had gone uncommonly quiet. Nate was more likely to hear if something snuck up on him, but he must keep his senses strained to their utmost. The problem was, he couldn't stay alert. The alternating bouts of cold and hot befuddled him, and weakened his body. Staying conscious was a feat in itself. Staying alert every second was impossible.

Nate plodded ever lower, a turtle propped on a stick. His buckskins became damp with sweat. Cramps spiked his good leg, and he had to stop twice to lift his foot and pump the leg until the cramps went away.

The whole while, Nate wondered where the wolverine had gotten to. It was bound to attack again. It had tasted his blood and eaten his flesh, and it would want a second helping.

Maybe, Nate reflected, this was the night his luck ran out. He had always known it would eventually. No one lived forever. In the wilderness, few even made it past fifty. Shakespeare was a rare exception.

Nate would prefer to die peaceably in bed with Winona at his side, but the wilderness was no respecter of wishes. It was a seething cauldron of violence in which all things came to an end and had no say over when that end would be.

How ironic, Nate mused. All that most people, white or red, wanted out of life was to live happily and contentedly to what the whites called a ripe old age, but life denied most the opportunity. Humans were born but to die. From the moment they came squalling into the world, each and every minute they lived was another minute nearer their grave. They were inexorably, inevitably destined to expire, and there was not a thing they could do about it.

If he could not die in bed, Nate would like die in a blaze of battle, to have his life ended quickly by hot lead or cold steel, or fangs and claws, if it came to that.

Nate chuckled. Here he was, barely able to stay conscious, a shadow of his robust self, a wolverine stalking him, and what was he doing? Reflecting on the vagaries of life and the grim certainty of death. Winona always said he thought too much, and she was right.

Not that Nate could help it. He had always been a thinker. Even when young, when most boys were out playing and roughhousing, he much preferred reading and pondering. He enjoyed feeding his mind as much as feeding his body. There was so much to learn, so much to know, no one person could never absorb it all in a lifetime. Yet another irony. By the time most folks were old enough and seasoned enough to have some sense of what life was about, they were knocking at death's door.

Life was one contradiction after another. Pain and pleasure. Love and hate. Happiness and sorrow. For every good aspect there was a bad, and both were dispensed in equal measure with no regard for anyone's welfare.

Nate breathed deep, filling his lungs with the crisp mountain air. It temporarily invigorated him. Lord, but he loved being alive! People who felt otherwise perplexed him, yet many did. To them life was a hollow, empty existence. To him it was a fountain of wonder.

If Nate's time *had* come, if this was to be his last night on earth, he had no regrets. He had savored life to the fullest. His civilized brethren were content to shuffle from cradle to grave in a daily grind of boredom, but not him. He had shattered his shackles. He had lived free, truly free, and gone places few others had gone, seen things few others had beheld.

Nate's only regret was that he might die without seeing his family again. Winona, Evelyn and Zach were everything to him. No man ever had a more caring wife, or children more worthy of respect. Sure, they had their faults. Everyone did. Winona carped too much. Zach was a hothead. Evelyn had an independent streak a mile wide. But he loved them and they loved him, and in the scheme of creation, was there anything that mattered more than love?

A bead of sweat trickled into Nate's left eye. The eye stung and watered, and he blinked it to clear his vision.

His mind was wandering too much. It was more fitting to think about the meaning of life and death and love in the comfort of his rocking chair in front of the hearth, not here, not now, not with his body ravaged and him easy prey for the devil incarnate that was stalking him.

Nate stopped and scanned his vicinity. The wolverine had to be there somewhere, watching and waiting. But waiting for what? The answer hit him like a hard punch to the gut.

Predators were not stupid. They did not put themselves at risk when there was no need. Wolves would cripple an elk and follow it until it grew so weak from loss of blood that it collapsed and could not fight back when they closed in. Coyotes did the same with small deer. Rattlesnakes bit prey and waited for the venom to take effect before swallowing their catch whole.

The wolverine knew Nate was badly hurt. It knew he had lost a lot of blood and was weakening. It was waiting for him to drop so it could feed on him without him resisting.

"Damned clever," Nate said aloud, and was startled by his voice. He did not sound like himself. He sounded like someone who had been to hell and back. "Where are you, you bastard?"

Predictably, there was no response, no growl, no snarl, nothing.

Nate laughed at how silly he was being, and once he

started, he could not stop. He laughed until his sides hurt and an invisible troll was beating on his head with an invisible hammer.

Suddenly Nate stopped. He was acting childish. Lapses like the bout of laughter could get him killed. It was so unlike him that the only explanation were the bites. Not only had they made him lightheaded and dizzy, they were affecting him in unforeseen ways.

Nate continued hiking. He swung his makeshift crutch to avoid a pine and put all his weight on his good leg. It was holding up, thank God, but he must go easy or he would exhaust himself long before he reached the bottom of the mountain. Yet another irony; he *couldn't* take it easy, not with the glutton after him.

"Damned if I do, damned if I don't," Nate said, and clamped his mouth shut. Talking to himself was another thing he must not do.

An owl hooted, reminding Nate that creatures besides the wolverine were abroad. With dried blood all over him, he was a lure for every meat eater for half a mile around.

Nate adopted a rhythm: lift the Hawken; swing the Hawken; take a step. Lift the Hawken; swing the Hawken; take a step. Over and over, until he performed the monotonous movements mechanically.

His body became one continual ache. His mind dulled to where his eyelids drooped. He felt his chin dip to his chest and snapped his head up. He must not pass out. He must not give up. Think of Winona! he inwardly shouted. Think of Winona and Evelyn and Zach and Lou and the McNairs.

But God, Nate was tired. Losing so much blood had drained his vitality. He was a shell of his usual self, an exhausted husk animated by a spark, and the spark was fading.

He lifted the Hawken; he swung the Hawken; he took a step.

A hiss roused Nate out of his stupor. It sounded like a dozen angry rattlesnakes venting their anger. Bracing himself on the rifle, he turned as fast as he could without tripping.

The wolverine had finally deigned to come out of the shadows. Powerful body coiled, it bared its fangs. The glutton had sensed that its quarry was close to collapsing and intended to hasten the collapse along.

Nate smiled grimly. "So there you are! Make buzzard bait of me if you can." So saying, he raised his pistol and squeezed the trigger. Nothing happened, other than a loud *click*. A misfire. He remembered the wolverine wrenching the pistol from his grasp back at the bluff, and he realized, in dismay, that he had neglected to check it afterward.

The wolverine snarled. A few more seconds, and it exploded toward him.

Nate did the only thing he could; he hurled the useless pistol at the glutton's head. He missed, but it forced the wolverine to dodge, gaining Nate the instant he needed to draw his other pistol. He cocked the flintlock as his arm rose.

The wolverine launched itself through the air, and Nate fired. The blast, the the spurt of smoke and flame, were simultaneous. The ball cored the wolverine high in the shoulder and spun it half around. It landed like a cat on all fours, snarled fiercely, and in a twinkling vanished into the greenery.

Nate stared in incredulous disbelief. His rifle was useless, his pistols spent. The tomahawk and bowie knife were at his waist but in his weakened state, he could not wield them effectively. The glutton had him at its mercy but unwittingly gave him a reprieve.

"Idiot," Nate said, and giggled giddily. Suddenly his lightheadedness worsened, and his knees threatened to give out. Relying on his crutch, he pivoted and hurried off as fast as he could hobble. As he went, he reloaded the flintlocks. His fingers were as sluggish as his brain, and it took much longer than it should have, much longer than was safe.

As he reloaded, Nate castigated himself. He was the idiot, not the wolverine. Instead of wearing himself down to the point where he was helpless, he should find somewhere to rest for a while, somewhere the wolverine could not get at him. Which was easier contemplated than done, especially in the dark. Climbing a tree was out of the question. He was too weak. A convenient cave would do him, but so far as he knew there were no caves anywhere in the valley.

What to do? What to do?

The excitement of confronting the wolverine had lent Nate a temporary boost of energy. He traveled over a hundred yards before his legs protested. He forged on. The wolverine was injured, but it would not stay away forever. When it grew hungry enough, it would take up where it had left off.

Nate suffered bouts of burning hot alternated by bouts of icy cold. One minute it felt like the temperature was a hundred and twenty, the next it felt as if it were the middle of winter.

A twig crunched to Nate's right. He spun, and the

Hawken fell. Without its support he tottered, and he placed his right foot flat on the ground to regain his balance. It was the wrong thing to do. His leg exploded in agony. It buckled, and he fell to his hands and knees.

Expecting the glutton to hurtle out of the undergrowth, Nate grabbed the Hawken and hastily pushed erect. He was surprised the wolverine did not attack. Maybe it wanted him so weak, he could not stand.

A quarter of an hour went by. The steep slope gave way to one less so. The pines merged into cottonwoods, and cottonwoods were a sign of water.

Sure enough, Nate soon heard a sustained gurgle. He hobbled faster, grinning when he broke from cover and beheld the darkly glimmering surface of one of the several streams that fed the lake. He moved briskly to its grassy edge, sank wearily onto his good knee, and eagerly cupped his hands.

Nate was hard pressed to recollect a time when water tasted so delicious. He drank several mouthfuls, then stopped to avoid upsetting his stomach. After glancing about to ensure it was safe, he plunged his entire head in, but only for a few seconds. Dripping wet from the neck up, he leaned back on his haunches and shook his head, spraying drops every which way.

It felt so good, Nate wanted to plunge his head in again. But he should not tempt an early grave twice. Instead, he loosened his buckskin shirt and splashed water down his chest. Goose bumps sprouted, and he shivered.

Across the stream the brush rustled and popped. Something was coming toward him, and coming fast.

Nate extended his arm and sighted down the pistol.

David Thompson

He could not hold it completely steady, so he used both hands.

The crackling grew louder. It could not be the wolverine because the wolverine was behind him. It was another of the night's denizens, a meat eater perhaps, that had caught Nate's blood-drenched scent and pegged him as dinner.

A silhouette took shape. Whatever it was, it was much larger than the wolverine. Breaking into the open, it charged straight toward him.

CHAPTER FIFTEEN

Shakespeare McNair centered his rifle on the wolverine that had been limping. Another shot might bring it down permanently. But as his finger tightened on the trigger, both gluttons sprang toward the spruce. He swung the muzzle but the wolverines were under the spruce before he could squeeze off a shot.

Shakespeare could not see them for all the limbs. He could hear them, though, sniffing and growling. He chided himself for not firing sooner. Now they had him treed. He figured they would wait him out. Sooner or later hunger or thirst would drive him down. But he failed to take into account the persistence for which gluttons were famous.

Wolverines never gave up. They never backed down. They never let prey escape. When they wanted to kill something, they killed it. When they wanted to help themselves to prey slain by other predators, they did;

149

there were reports of wolverines driving grizzlies off kills.

When loud scratching rose from below, Shakespeare's brow knit in consternation. He assumed the gluttons were digging their claws into the trunk, marking the tree as bears were wont to do. Then the spruce shook slightly, and some of the lower branches rustled and swayed.

Sweat broke out all over Shakespeare's body. The wolverines weren't *scratching* the spruce, they were *climbing* it.

Suddenly Shakespeare's brainstorm did not seem so brilliant. Wolverines were at home in trees. They often waited on branches to pounce on unwary prey. They were good climbers. Surprisingly agile, given their size, and certainly better climbers then he was.

The bottom half of the spruce was shrouded in darkness. Shakespeare shifted but could not spot them.

"Consarn these critters to Hades," Shakespeare fumed. He was mad at himself, not them, for being such a dunderhead.

Another growl gave him an inkling of how close they were.

Shakespeare probed the branches. He peered behind the trunk. They could be anywhere. He started to rise so he could watch both sides of the tree at once. He forgot charred limbs made for precarious footing. His left foot slipped, and he clutched the trunk to keep from falling. He almost dropped the Hawken.

There was a savage snarl, and a feral face materialized out of the dark. Razor teeth snapped at Shakespeare's leg, and missed. He pointed his rifle but the wolverine disappeared.

Shakespeare decided to stir things up. If he could rile them, it might provoke them into trying to get him and he could blast them into oblivion. Accordingly, he gripped the nearest charred branch and twisted, but it was too strong. He tried another. A *crack* rewarded his effort. The piece was ten inches long. He broke it into thirds and threw one of the pieces at where he had seen the wolverine. Clattering resulted as the stick dropped from limb to limb and ultimately struck the ground.

Shakespeare tried again. He threw a piece to the left of the first. Again there was the clack of wood on wood but nothing else. Disappointed, Shakespeare threw the last piece to the right.

Almost immediately, a rumbling growl arose. Quickly, Shakespeare broke off another limb, broke it, and threw the largest piece. Another growl heralded sudden scrambling and a wolverine appeared almost at his feet.

Claws sheared at his leg. Shakespeare jerked his leg aside, pointed the Hawken straight down, and fired. At that range, he should have blown the glutton's brains out. But the beast moved and the ball thudded into the trunk.

Again it disappeared among the boughs.

His fingers flying, Shakespeare commenced to reload. That had not gone as well as he hoped. Stirring the wolverines up was easy enough but shooting them was not. They were too incredibly fast.

Shakespeare uncapped his powder horn and carefully poured the proper amount of powder down the Hawken's muzzle. Some of the black grains spilled. Not a lot, but enough, evidently, that there was a loud sneeze.

"Bless you," Shakespeare said. He chortled, then paraphrased, "I should not laugh, for fear of opening my lips and receiving thy reek."

A limb lower down moved. Then the one next to it, and the one next to that. One after the other in a half circle, until the swaying stopped at a limb on the other side of the tree.

"Tricky devils," Shakespeare complimented them. "Two directions at once, is that your intent? Well, you won't find me napping." He wrapped a ball in a patch, thumbed both into the end of the barrel, and slid the ramrod from its housing. "Just hold your horses another thirty seconds so I can treat you to the reception you deserve." He applied the ramrod.

Movement signified the wolverines were about to tear him from his roost. Shakespeare kept glancing from one side of the spruce to the other, unsure which animal would try for him first. He finished reloading and held the Hawken ready.

"What are you waiting for, you whoreson scurvy vermin?" Shakespeare taunted. "Your greatest want is you want much of meat. Why should you want? Behold, the earth hath roots. Within this mile break forth a hundred springs. The oaks bear mast, the briars scarlet hips. The bounteous housewife, nature, on each bush lays her full mess before you. Want! Why want?"

The gluttons stayed silent.

"What's this, then?" Shakespeare said. "Does a Skunk Bear have your tongue?" He tittered gleefully. "But I shouldn't blame you, should I, when you are only doing what wolverines do." He quoted more William S. "A beastly ambition, which the gods grant thee to attain to. If thou wert the lion, the fox would beguile thee; If

thou wert the lamb, the fox would eat thee; if thou wert
the fox, the lion would suspect thee, when peradventure
thou wert accused by the ass; if thou wert the ass, thy
dullness would torment thee, and still thou livedst but
as a breakfast for the wolf; if thou wert the wolf, thy
greediness would afflict thee." He paused. "Not that
wolves are any more greedy than you two bastards."

There was no movement anywhere.

"According to the fair play of the world, let me have
an audience." Shakespeare tossed down a verbal gaunt-
let. "Then let the earth be drunken with our blood!"

As if that were their cue, the wolverines streaked toward him, one up the near side, the other up the far
side. They climbed with the facility of squirrels, spring-
ing from limb to limb.

Shakespeare sighted down the barrel, and fired. The
glutton about to rend his legs stopped in mid leap as if it
had charged into an invisible wall. It fell back, bounced
off a branch, and plummeted from sight.

That left the other. Palming his pistol, Shakespeare
whirled. It was almost on him, its claws raking the
trunk for purchase. He leaned down to be sure he
would not miss, shoving the flintlock at the wolverine's
eyes. He smiled as he fired, thinking his nightmare was
over.

The sound of the branch under him breaking was lost
in the boom of the pistol. Shakespeare dropped feet
first. He glimpsed gleaming eyes and tapered teeth. His
right heel struck a limb and he tumbled into space. An
illusion, for there were so many branches, he careened
into one after another. He lost his sense of which way
was up and which way was down.

A tremendous blow to Shakespeare's gut caused the world to wink out of existence. When it winked back again, he was on his belly over a limb, his arms and legs dangling. His entire body was a welter of pain.

Shakespeare raised his head. He had lost his rifle. He had lost his pistol. He had nearly lost his life. A slight sound alerted him to a furry form descending rapidly toward him. The sight galvanized him into placing his hands on the limb and swinging his legs up to straddle it. He swooped a hand to his waist, fearing he had lost his knife, but the bone handle molded to his fingers just as the wolverine came to the branch he was on and started toward him.

Shakespeare waited until the glutton was so close he could see its nostrils flare, and swung. The tip of the blade sliced into its neck as, with lightning swiftness, the wolverine sprang back out of reach.

Snarling, the glutton crouched and fixed him with its baleful eyes. If ever a creature craved his life, this was the one.

Shakespeare held the knife point out. He could not move with the wolverine so near. He waited for it to do something, anything, but strangely enough all it did was stare.

Then a bough behind Shakespeare bent and bounced with a heavy weight, and as he glanced around, out of the murk came the second wolverine. They had suckered him, and now had him between them.

Shakespeare gingerly shifted. He had one on the right and one on the left and only his knife with which to defend himself. It hardly seemed adequate. The Hawken had not slain them. The pistol had not slain them. *What did it take?* he asked himself. *A cannon? A keg of powder to blow them to bits?* He remembered an old French trapper telling him wolverines were impossible to kill, and that Frenchman might have been right.

As if they had communicated by some silent signal, the gluttons began to slink toward him.

To stay in the spruce was certain death. Shakespeare feinted at one wolverine, feinted at the other, then slid the knife into its sheath and dropped feet first from the branch. As he fell he grabbed another branch a few feet lower down and from there swung to another. He spied the carpet of needles through a gap, and letting go, he dropped the rest of the way. He tried to land like a cat but he came down slightly off balance and spilled onto his chest and shoulder.

Overhead, claws clacked on bark.

Shakespeare did not look up. He ran. He darted into the undergrowth and sprinted for his life. If he lived he would come back and search for his Hawken and flintlock.

Growls of rage followed him. A thud warned him one of the wolverines had jumped to the ground. Seconds later the other wolverine joined its sibling.

Since they could trail him using their noses alone and Shakespeare had no way of masking his scent, he made no pretense at stealth. He crashed headlong through the brush, his sole goal to put as much distance between him and his fierce pursuers as he could. He did not hear them chasing him but they had to be.

Shakespeare had a shred of hope to cling to. He had shot both—or else shot one twice, he was not entirely sure—and their wounds might slow them. He was counting on that. Otherwise, they would overtake him before he went half a mile. He would fight them with his dying breath, but the outcome was foreordained.

Shakespeare thought of Blue Water Woman. He would like his last moments on earth to be spent thinking about her. She was the love of his life, and it was a tragic shame they had not wed sooner. That they came together at all was a joy beyond words, even for the Bard.

A boulder hove out of nowhere. Shakespeare veered to avoid it and his foot hit a rock or a root. Down he went. His right elbow struck the boulder, jarring his arm so severely, the knife arced from fingers gone numb. Frantic, Shakespeare crawled after it. He ran his other hand over the spot where he thought it fell but he could not find it. "No!" he whispered. "No! No! No!"

From somewhere to his rear rasped a growl.

Shakespeare pumped into motion, running full-out. A tide of dismay washed over him. The knife had been his last means of defending himself. He did not carry a tomahawk, like Nate and Zach. Without a weapon he stood no prayer whatsoever. As he ran he cast about for a tree limb, a long limb, as thick as a spear, but spotted none that fit his urgent need.

Suddenly Shakespeare realized that in all the confusion he had become turned around, and was running north instead of east. Not that the direction was important. The wolverines would pursue him no matter where he went.

Waiting in the spruce to ambush them had turned out to be a possibly fatal mistake. Sometimes that happened. Sometimes a person did the best he could and it was not enough.

That was part of the reason Shakespeare liked the Bard so much. The original William S. wrote a lot of tragedies, which was fitting since in Shakespeare's estimation life itself always had a tragic ending; everyone died. People were born and learned and loved and laughed and did all the things people do, and then they died.

To what end? Shakespeare echoed the Bard. Life was like a present wrapped in pink ribbon. You opened it thinking you had a wonderful surprise in store, and the wonderful surprise was the grave.

The Almighty had a strange sense of humor.

A pain in Shakespeare's side forced him to slow and ended his mental meanderings. He was not a young man anymore. He could only do so much before his body objected.

The pines were thinning. So was the underbrush. Shakespeare was glad in one respect; he could make better time. But if he could, so could the wolverines. He checked over his shoulder for the tenth time in as many minutes but did not see them. He liked to think they had given up, but he knew that was wishful thinking.

Shakespeare was beginning to wonder about the wisdom of moving to the new valley. First they had clashed with a grizzly. Now they were up to their necks in wolverines. What next? Yes, the valley was everything Nate had promised. Yes, it was lush with timber and teeming with game. Yes, it was a genuine paradise. But every paradise had its hellish underbelly.

In that respect the new valley was no different from the rest of the Rockies. Vast regions were unexplored. Thousands of square miles were overrun with a multitude of wild creatures. Many of those creatures were harmless, many others were not. The new valley had its share of both.

When he was younger, Shakespeare did not mind the meat eaters so much. He accepted them as a matter of course, as part and parcel of life in the wilderness. But now that he was getting on in years, he could do without being eaten. He would like to live out his days in ease and serenity.

Up ahead, deciduous trees appeared. Among them might be a fallen branch Shakespeare could use. He tried to go faster but his side refused.

Shakespeare came to a belt of brush and slogged through it rather than go around. He glanced back but the gluttons were still not in sight. It never occurred to him they might have sped ahead of him and were waiting; not until he broke into the open and spied a crouched figure ready to pounce.

CHAPTER SIXTEEN

Zach King raised his head off the ground. Only a few feet away crouched a dusky wolverine. The animal had ripped his leg open as Zach fell. Now it bared its teeth, hissed and sprang.

It happened so fast, so unexpectedly, that for once Zach's reflexes failed him. The wolverine was on him before he could rise. He flung out a hand to protect his neck, but that would not stop a glutton.

Something else did. A rifle stock swept from above and slammed into the wolverine's head, knocking it sideways. The beast recovered instantly, and snarled at the rifle's wielder.

Lou had reacted without thinking, and did so again. She started to reverse her grip so she could shoot. She glanced down at her rifle as she did, and in that brief heartbeat, a bristly bulk slammed into her, bowling her over. Teeth went for her jugular. The only thing that

159

saved her was that by sheer chance she was holding her
Hawken between her body and the wolverine's, and the
barrel was across her throat, preventing the wolverine
from tearing it open.

The sight of Lou on the ground with the wolverine on
top of her brought rage boiling up out of Zach. He always had a temper, and few things set his temper off
like that of a loved one in danger. Molten quicksilver, he
threw himself at the glutton, smashing into it and driving it off her. His left arm looped around its neck as his
right swooped to his waist, and the hilt of his bowie.

Locked together, Zach and the wolverine rolled and
tumbled, Zach striving to free his knife, which had
snagged in his buckskin shirt and would not slide from
its sheath, and the wolverine striving to get at Zach with
its teeth and claws.

They came to a stop. Zach pushed clear and leaped
up, the bowie in his hand. Simultaneously, the wolverine regained its footing and without any hesitation
charged.

"Zach!" Lou cried, jerking her rifle to her shoulder
and pressing her thumb on the hammer. But she was not
quick enough. The two of them merged into a furiously
battling whirlwind.

Zach had braced his legs as the wolverine rushed him
but the brute force of its rush smashed him onto his
back. He managed to clamp the fingers of his left hand
on the wolverine's throat to keep its snapping teeth
from his own. But he could not stop its claws from tearing at his buckskins.

Bunching his shoulders, Zach stabbed the bowie
deep. Once, twice, three times the steel sank to the hilt,
but it appeared to have no effect. He flung back his arm

to stab again, and suddenly the earth under them dissolved into thin air. For a few harrowing moments Zach thought they had gone over the edge of a cliff, but it was only a drop-off of some fifteen to twenty feet.

Zach hit hard on his shoulder, and shoved. He was vaguely aware that they were on a narrow shelf, and that beyond lay a slope. He pushed upright as the glutton rose and crouched for another assault.

"Come and get me, you son of a bitch!"

A rifle cracked, and a lead ball kicked up a dirt geyser inches from the wolverine's head.

Lou could not believe she had missed. She streaked her fingers to a pistol swifter than they ever streaked before, but once again, it was not swift enough.

In an explosion of raw ferocity, the enraged wolverine tore into Zach. Zach locked his fingers on its throat as it drove him toward the drop-off. He tried to push it away, but its claws were hooked in his shirt. He turned—or tried to—and tripped over his own feet.

Zach was in trouble. His back was pinned to the drop-off. He could not move freely, and the wolverine's jaws would soon reach his neck. He tried to hurl it off but could not.

Lou pointed her pistol. Deathly afraid she would hit her husband instead of the glutton, she held her fire. "Zach! Break free!"

Zach heard her, and in the recesses of his mind a tiny voice angrily roared, *What do you think I am trying to do, woman!* But he did not reply. Every iota of his being was focused on not letting the wolverine's slavering fangs reach him. To that end, and to gain space, he thrust the soles of his moccasins against the drop-off, and pushed. As it happened, at the same instant the wolverine gave a powerful wrench that started them rolling, and once they started, they could not stop. They came to the brink of the slope and hurtled over it. Gravity took over. Faster and faster and faster they rolled, the wolverine slashing and snapping, Zach doing his utmost to stay alive.

He buried the bowie to the crossguard and went to yank it out. Suddenly a boulder was in front of them. It was not large, no more than waist high and a couple of feet in length, but they were rolling so fast and hit the boulder so hard, the result was akin to being struck by a cannonball.

Zach was propelled in one direction, the wolverine in another. Pain flooded Zach's chest and shot up his left arm to his shoulder. He lost all control, and bounced down the slope like a disjointed child's doll, his arms and legs flapping, unable to arrest his descent. It seemed to go on and on and on, until every sinew and every bone hurt and he felt half sick.

Then, abruptly, Zach came to a stop. He was on his left side facing a dark wall of forest. Twice he tried to sit up. Twice his arms would not work. Finally he made it. Glancing over his shoulder, he marveled at how high the slope was. Other boulders besides the one they had struck sprinkled it from end to end. He was fortunate to be breathing.

Zach smiled, but the smile died as he realized that the wolverine must still be alive, too, and if so, it would take up where they left off.

Hardly had the thought flitted through Zach's mind than a stygian shape rippled toward him, impetus to scramble erect and reach for the weapons at his waist.

But they were gone; his tomahawk, the pistols, he had lost them in the fall.

The wolverine stopped a dozen feet away and tilted its head from side to side as if examining him.

"Want to call it a draw and try again another time?" Zach asked, and was answered with a snarl. "I didn't think so."

Like a cougar stalking a fawn, the wolverine circled, its eyes never leaving Zach's face.

Zach edged toward the trees. If he could get his hands on a club, he would go down swinging. But the wolverine suddenly darted between him and the woods. Crafty devil that it was, it wanted him in the open.

Just then shouts wafted from on high. Lou was calling his name. Zach cupped a hand to his mouth to let her know where he was, but the movement provoked the glutton into throwing itself at him with twice the savagery.

This time Zach stayed on his feet. He got both arms up, his fingers enfolding fur. The wolverine attempted to bite him, but he thrust it at forearm's length. Claws raked his wrist, his abdomen. He could not hold it there forever. With an oath, he threw it to the ground, but it was back up in flash and on him before he could catch his breath. Down they went.

A mouth full of spikes clamped onto Zach's left arm. He cried out, and sought to pry the wolverine's jaws off. When that did not work, he punched it. When that had no effect, he clutched at its side, seeking to push it away. His hand brushed something hard, something stuck in the wolverine's ribs. Elated, he pulled, and had the dripping bowie secure in his fist.

The wolverine bounded back and uttered a new cry, not a growl or a snarl but a high-pitched sound Zach had not heard it make before, a challenge, perhaps, or a call to others of its kind. The notion jolted him. According to his father, there were three or four wolverines, all told. If another heard the cry and came to help this one—

Zach did not finish the thought. He must end the fight quickly, and not just because another glutton might show up. His arms, his legs, his chest, had all been ripped repeatedly by the wolverine's claws. Some of the cuts were deep, and bleeding profusely. He was tired and weakening and could not hold his own much longer.

So Zach did the last thing the wolverine would expect. *He* attacked *it*. Dashing in close, he speared the bowie at the glutton's neck but it nimbly leaped aside. Zach slashed sideways and opened the wolverine's shoulder. Unfazed, the wolverine raked its claws at Zach's leg, and it was Zach's turn to spring out of the way.

They faced one another, man pitted against beast in the most primeval of conflicts; brain and muscle against sinew and savagery. It was kill or be killed, the survival of the fittest, and how to survive was one lesson Zach King had learned well over his two decades in the wilderness.

Now, as the wolverine crouched to attack, Zach crouched to meet it. Lou's shouts were growing louder, but he did not let them distract him. He must concentrate on the wolverine and only the wolverine.

The demon crossed the space separating them. Zach

swung, but the wolverine ducked under his blade. Teeth found his thigh, and ripped. In return he lanced the bowie at the wolverine's back. The tip glanced off bone, digging a furrow in the hide but doing no damage to its vitals.

The wound drove the glutton berserk.

Zach barely had time to set himself, and the carnivore was on him. He stabbed and scored when the wolverine was in mid leap. Grappling, they fell and thrashed about in a wild melee of blood and blade and teeth and claws.

Zach fought with an urgency born of self-preservation, yet even that might not be enough. He was being bitten and clawed to ribbons. He buried the bowie for the eighth or ninth time but he might as well have been stabbing pudding.

In the heat of their frenzied combat, Zach became disoriented. He had no inkling they were near the trees until they suddenly rolled in among them. They passed under a pine and rolled into a thicket. A limb pricked Zach's cheek. Another nearly took out an eye.

Zach became a madman. He *must* slay the wolverine. It must not remain a threat to those he loved. He weaved the bowie in a steel tapestry of silver and scarlet. They came apart, and the wolverine was first up. It leaped, and Zach met it with a well-placed foot, flipping the glutton away from him.

Zach rose to meet its next rush, but it did not reappear. Wary of a trick, he stayed where he was. Let it come to him. He hefted the bowie.

Time gave the illusion of standing still. Not a leaf stirred, not a twig cracked. When more than a minute elapsed and he was not set upon, Zach slowly unfurled.

Suddenly the brush behind him crackled. He whirled but it wasn't the wolverine. "Lou," he breathed. "Be careful."

"Where is it?" Louisa asked. She had been beside herself with fear when Zach and the creature catapulted down the mountain. Breathless from running, she gripped his arm. Her fingers grew damp with blood. Only then did she notice how badly his buckskins were torn, and the dark stain of the score of claw marks underneath. "Dear God! Look at you!"

"Forget that." Zach snatched one of her pistols and cocked it. "The thing is still alive. Be ready."

Lou leveled her Hawken. "Where did it get to?"

"Your guess is as good as mine." Zach sensed it was near, very near, but now that Lou was there, it was wary.

Lou was appalled. Not by the likelihood of being attacked, but by what the wolverine had done to the man she loved. His shirt was shredded, his pants little better. "We can't just stand here! You're bleeding to death."

"I'll be all right," Zach assured her. He had lost a lot of blood but not so much that he could not do what needed to be done.

"Let's get you to water," Lou pleaded. "I'll clean your wounds and bandage you."

"Forget about me. Pay attention to the woods."

"The wolverine can wait! It's you I'm worried about. Quit being so stubborn!" Lou was practically beside herself.

"Women!" Zach muttered. She could not have picked a worse moment to make a fuss. "Why is it you never listen?"

"Men!" Lou retorted. "And I'm listening just fine, to a kettle calling a pot black." She reached for him. "Please. Let's get out of here."

Zach gestured angrily. "It's not safe, damn it!"

That was when a fierce beast hurtled from the dark. Lou tried to bring her rifle to bear, but the glutton slammed into her, smashing her against Zach, and both she and Zach went down, she on her back with the wolverine on top of her and about to bite her face.

Louisa screamed.

"*Nooooo!*" Zach swung the pistol with all his strength, clubbing the wolverine across the skull. He did not knock it down but he did knock it off Lou. It coiled as he fired and put a ball into its body about where the heart should be. He must have missed because the shot did not slow it down. It did divert the glutton, though, from his wife to him. He tried to club it but it dodged, and once again he was embroiled in a claw-and-steel struggle for his life.

Lou jumped up to help. The Hawken had gone flying when the wolverine attacked her, and stooping, she desperately searched for it. "Where?" she cried in despair. "Where did it get to?"

Zach sliced his bowie into the glutton's belly. He had stabbed it so many times that its hair was matted with blood, yet it still refused to die. He stabbed it again, lower down, and in doing so, exposed his neck and shoulders. The wolverine capitalized by sinking its teeth into his right shoulder clear down to the shoulder blade. Inadvertently, Zach dropped the bowie.

Lou saw Zach stiffen in agony, saw blood spurt from his shoulder. She also saw the wolverine shift to bite Zach in the neck just as her fingers closed on the Hawken.

The wolverine had Zach at its mercy but it paused and snarled. That pause proved crucial. It bought Lou the seconds she needed to jam the Hawken's muzzle against the wolverine's ear and stroke the trigger.

Hair, bone and brains spattered Zach. He shoved the glutton off and sank wearily onto his back. He had enough strength left to grin. "It looks like women are good for something after all."

"Which is more than women can say about men." Lou chuckled and hunkered next to him. Awash in relief, she tenderly touched his cheek. "We were lucky."

"No," Zach said. "We were damned lucky."

CHAPTER SEVENTEEN

Nate King was burning up with fever. He was constantly light-headed and weak. In his near-delirious state, he attributed the apparition running toward him to a be figment of his imagination, and blurted, "Now I'm seeing things."

Shakespeare McNair came to a stop on the other side of the stream and bent over with his hands on his knees. "I'm as real as you are, Horatio," he wheezed. "Pinch me and I'll yelp." He sucked air deep into his aching lungs. "You are a wonderful sight for this old coon's eyes, hoss."

"You're real?" Nate repeated, and rose unsteadily. "It's not the fever?" Emotion gripped him, and he tottered.

Concern etched Shakespeare's weathered visage. "What's wrong?" He waded across and took Nate by the shoulders. "You look about done in."

"I have a wolverine after me."

"Only one?"

"What?"

I have two after me," Shakespeare revealed. "It must be they think I'm tastier." His surrogate son did not grin at his joke, which was a sign how bad off Nate must be. "Where's your horse? I managed to lose mine."

"Same here. I'm afoot." The dizziness returned, and Nate hobbled toward a boulder to sit. "I need to rest."

Shakespeare helped him, saying, "As mountain men, we would make fine store clerks. We have not so much brains as ear wax." Squatting, he examined Nate's leg and the tourniquet. "No wonder you are nearly out on your feet. You might want to keep in mind, Horatio, that when you are attacked by wild animals, the general idea is to *not* let them bite you."

Nate mustered a wan grin. "Why didn't you tell me sooner? Here I thought it was to let them eat me alive." A spasm racked him, and he closed his eyes and lowered his chin to his chest. "I don't mind admitting I am about done in."

"I'll take care of you," Shakespeare said quietly. He could not say it louder for the lump in his throat. "That is, if you don't mind lending me your rifle. I seem to have misplaced my guns and my knife."

"How's that?" Nate looked up, and smirked. "You might want to keep in mind that when you are attacked by wild animals, the general idea is to hold on to your weapons."

"I would beat you with a tree if I had one handy." Shakespeare patted the Hawken. "Let me have it and I will keep watch while you rest."

"It's broken," Nate said.

"Not exactly our finest hour, is it?" Shakespeare helped himself to a pistol. "These will have to do us, then. And I would be obliged for the loan of your tomahawk."

"Help yourself. I can't hardly swing it, anyway." Nate leaned on the Hawken, his forehead against the barrel. It felt wonderfully cool on his skin.

Shakespeare gazed skyward. "What is the o'clock?" he quoted. "Not yet midnight, if I know my North Stars, and I do. Here I reckoned it must be nigh on dawn."

"They will come for us before daylight," Nate predicted.

"They are here."

A growl wafted from out of the undergrowth to the west. Seconds later it was answered to the north. A series of cries was exchanged, their significance as elusive as the wolverines.

"A family reunion," Shakespeare remarked. "How touching. I always thought Skunk Bears had no feelings. It just goes to show that all creatures are daffodils at heart."

"Do I have the fever, or do you?"

"You are hilarious, sir," Shakespeare said, "and would be more so if you had a sense of humor."

"No fair," Nate said, "picking on a man who can hardly think."

"You make it too easy, but I'll let that one pass." Shakespeare wagged his pistol at a bank overlooking a pool. "There is where we should make our stand. They can't get at us except from one direction unless they're partial to a late night swim."

"I trust your judgment." Nate attempted to stand, but his traitorous legs would not cooperate. "Damn. I won't be of much use."

"Use is relative." Shakespeare slipped an arm under Nate's. "If I need a distraction, I can always throw you to them and shoot them while they are busy eating you."

"It's nice to be good for something." Nate grunted as Shakespeare assisted his rise. He placed all his weight on the Hawken. "If you have to, put me down and run for it. I'll hold them off as long as I can."

Shakespeare started toward the bank. "Hold them how, exactly? By auctioning off your body parts to the highest bidder?"

"Where do you come up with stuff like that?" Nate marveled.

"When you have lived as long as I have, sprout, genius rolls trippingly off the tongue."

Carefully swinging his crutch, Nate responded, "One man's notion of a genius is another man's notion of a simpleton."

"You are not as helpless as you make yourself out to be." Shakespeare was enjoying their banter, but he was extremely worried. Nate needed doctoring. He had seen men die from infected bites: horrible, lingering deaths no human being should ever endure. He had to get Nate to the cabins, to Blue Water Woman and Winona. But first there was the little matter of the wolverines. Three of them, three of the fiercest creatures ever to trod God's green earth.

Shakespeare had been watching the forest and listening. From the stealthy sounds and furtive movement, he deduced the wolverines were up to something, and it would not be long before he found out exactly what.

Nate wobbled, and recovered. He was growing weaker. He sought to shrug it off but his usually indomitable will could not muster strength where there was none. He was enormously glad to have stumbled on Shakespeare, but enormously worried that Shakespeare would die protecting him. "I suppose I can't talk you into leaving me and going for help?"

"You are as transparent as glass, Horatio," the older man rejoined. "We live or die together. Friends forever, remember?"

"Blue Water Woman is right. You are a stubborn cuss."

"I take after her." Shakespeare guided Nate up the bank. "Easy does it. If you fall on me, you big ox, you'll break my leg."

The bank was eight feet high and about that wide, with a wall of earth on the side facing the pool. Shakespeare eased Nate down at the top but held on to the Hawken. "I'll keep this, if you don't mind."

"Suit yourself." Nate could not swing it hard enough to use effectively, anyway. He leaned over the edge. The pool was a good ten feet across. There was no telling how deep; four or five feet at the most. A man could wade across. A wolverine had to swim. "I'll watch this side."

"That was the idea." Shakespeare gripped the Hawken by the barrel and performed a practice swing. He tended to forget how heavy Hawkens were. The hardwood stock could crush a skull like an eggshell.

Down in the valley, the light in Nate's cabin window still burned bright. "Winona is up late tonight."

"What do you want to bet Blue Water Woman is there, and the two of them are calling us unladylike

173

names and comparing our intelligence to that of tree stumps?"

"I never bet the sun won't rise," Nate said.

Shakespeare laughed, or started to, but stopped when a four-legged form flowed out of the woods to the west. It was well out of pistol range so all he could do was watch as it stopped, raised its head, and stared fixedly at them. "We have company," he announced.

"It is a tad late for visitors to come calling," Nate quipped, seeking to make light of their plight.

"Some folks have no manners," Shakespeare responded. "They show up on your doorstep at any hour and expect you to be a fount of hospitality."

A second glutton emerged from cover to the south and came halfway to the stream before it, too, stopped.

"One more and the quadrille will commence," Shakespeare said, leaning the Hawken against his leg. "Or maybe I should call it a quintdrille." He chortled merrily. "It's too bad the rest of the world doesn't have an intellect as refined as mine."

"They do when they're drunk," Nate retorted.

Shakespeare glanced north, then east. *Which would it be?* he wondered, and had his answer when the third wolverine burst out of the vegetation to the north. This one did not stop. "It's do or die!" he hollered, and raised the pistol. But he did not fire. Not yet. He needed to be certain. He needed to wait until the wolverine was so close he could not miss.

Nate drew the other flintlock. When the wolverine to the north broke from cover, the wolverines to the south and the west bounded toward them. He had never heard of gluttons working in packs, but wolves and coyotes did it, so why not wolverines? He figured the one to the west would reach them first so he shifted toward it and took deliberate aim.

Shakespeare's mouth went dry. He had tangled with wolverines before but always singly, never so many at once. He fought an urge to take his eyes off the one charging him to check on Nate. *Stay calm*, he told himself, *and we will make it out alive.*

Nate's arm was shaking, he was so weak. He wrapped his other hand around the flintlock to steady it. Another bout of dizziness nearly caused him to pass out. He could not hold a bead on the wolverine if his life depended on it, and it did. Squinting in intense concentration, he licked his lips and drew back the hammer.

Another fifteen yards and Shakespeare would shoot. "Are you all right?" he asked over his shoulder without turning his head, and did not receive an answer. "Nate?" Torn between affection and necessity, he chose necessity. He had to. It would do Nate no good if he were dead. He held his arm perfectly still, and fired. It was as if the wolverine slammed into a wall. The glutton slumped to the ground, but the next second was back up and rushing toward McNair with cold bestial fury contorting its features.

Shakespeare shoved the pistol under his belt. He barely had time to raise the Hawken when the wolverine was on him. He swung, but only succeeded in driving it back a few feet. It hissed and lunged at his legs. Sidestepping, Shakespeare whipped the Hawken in a blow that ended with the stock connecting with the wolverine's head. That would be enough to drop most animals, but not the glutton. Undaunted, it lunged again.

Nate had not taken his eyes off the wolverine to the west, which had thirty yards to cover. Consequently, he was that much more surprised when loud splashing alerted him he had been wrong; the wolverine to the south was the faster of the two, and had reached the stream. He glanced down, and there it was, swimming across the pool with a speed that was disconcerting. It still had to scale the bank and might or might not reach him before the other one, but it was closer, and Nate swivelled and fired.

Clubbing a wolverine, Shakespeare had discovered, was a lot like swatting a fly on the wing; it took as much luck as anything else. He had swung the Hawken eight times and missed with every swing. The glutton darted right, it darted left, it leaped back out of reach. He kept after it, swinging, always swinging, to keep it away from Nate. Then a shot split the night, and despite himself, despite knowing he should not take his eyes off the wolverine, Shakespeare took his eyes off the wolverine to glance at Nate and ensure Nate was all right. It was only for an instant, but in that instant teeth sliced into Shakespeare's left leg.

Nate missed. He had aimed for the wolverine's head but cored its neck. Blood spurted from a ruptured vein and the glutton slowed, but only momentarily. Snarling and spitting, it reached the bank and clawed up it in a mad rage.

Nate set the pistol in his lap to free his hands so he could reload. He heard Shakespeare curse, heard the wolverine he had shot snarl. He did not look. He concentrated on the pistol instead. His only hope was to shoot the glutton again before it reached him. Powder, patch, ball, ramrod, he had done it a thousand times, but never as quickly as he did it now. He cocked the hammer and looked up as the wolverine scrambled over the rim. Its mouth was open, its teeth bared to rip and rend. Nate shoved the barrel into its mouth and squeezed the trigger.

This time Shakespeare knew better. He did not take his gaze from the glutton. But the wolverine tore its gaze from him. It glanced toward the sound of the shot, and finally, wonderful-as-could be finally, Shakespeare smashed the rifle against its head.

Nate set the flintlock in his lap and took hold of his powder horn. The third wolverine was flying along the stream toward him. It only had twenty feet to cover. He upended the horn over his left hand, pouring the powder into his palm. He had an entire handful when the wolverine launched itself at him, and with a sweep of his arm, Nate hurled the powder in the wolverine's face even as he threw himself onto his side. The wolverine sailed over him, alighted on all fours, and whirled.

Shakespeare swept the Hawken over his head. The glutton had sagged but it was not dead. Not yet. He smashed the stock down, again and again and again, stopping only when brains oozed from the split skull.

Nate drew his bowie. The wolverine was wheezing, sneezing and blinking, thanks to the powder in its mouth, nose and eyes. It glanced up as the bowie arced down, the razor edge nearly severing its neck from its body.

Whirling, Shakespeare raised the Hawken, stiffened in amazement, and slowly lowered it. "I'll be damned. Both of them?"

"I fight better when I'm sitting down."

"I think I will join you." Shakespeare sat and set the

blood-smeared Hawken beside him. "I do not mind admitting, Horatio, that I am getting too old for frolics like this."

"Darn. I was hoping we would wage war on the Blackfeet tomorrow."

"The only thing I want to wage war on is that bottle of whiskey I have hidden away. I figure I deserve to treat myself." Shakespeare glanced at the bite in his leg, and wearily sighed. "Do you know what the worst part of all this is?"

Nate nodded. "Our wives will never let us hear the end of it."

EPILOGUE

"Will you look at them?" Winona King said from the doorway of her cabin. "Loafing the day away yet again."

Blue Water Woman was placing plates on the table for supper. "Loafing is what men do best."

Over at the counter, Louisa was slicing a freshly baked loaf of bread. "They'll sure have a lot of chores to catch up on when their holiday is over."

All three women spoke loudly enough to be heard by the three men lounging in chairs out in the afternoon sun.

"Holiday?" Zach sputtered. He did not have a shirt on and was swathed in so many bandages, he resembled a mummy. "Does she think I *wanted* to sit around twiddling my thumbs the past two weeks? I'd rather be off in the mountains hunting or exploring."

"You need to learn to relax, young sir," Shakespeare advised, lazily stretching. "Learn to take things in stride, like me."

"Says the man who nearly killed himself going for help for me," Nate interjected. "Running all night and most of the next day. At your age!"

"It was more of a fast limp," Shakespeare said. "I just didn't want you dying on us. The comical stunts you pull keep me chuckling."

"Name one comical stunt."

"You came west to live in the Rockies."

Winona stepped over to Nate's side. "It will be half an hour yet before we eat. Is there anything I can get any of you?"

"A horse and a saddle," Zach said.

Nate held out his hand and Winona tenderly clasped it. "I have all I need right here."

Snickering, Shakespeare smacked his chair. "I declare. You two act like you are just wed. Sew your lips together, why don't you, and save yourselves all that puckering?"

"Wasn't he the one who rode all the way to Bent's Fort for a new mirror for Blue Water Woman for her birthday?" Nate mentioned.

"Yes, he was," Winona said. "He is also the one who brings her a bouquet of wild flowers nearly every day in the spring, when they bloom."

"I didn't know that."

"Oh, yes. Blue Water Woman says he is the most romantic man she has ever met or heard of."

Shakespeare was turning red. "Flatheads lie a lot."

"Should I tell her you said that?" Winona asked sweetly.

"Not unless you want to see me stomped to death." Shakespeare gestured at the hides stretched on wooden frames. "How are the rugs coming along?"

"There will be one for each cabin," Winona said. "The glutton Zach slew had too many holes in it."

Nate gazed toward the mountains. "All four are dead. That's the important thing. Our valley is safe again."

The sun had set when the big female came out of the den. As always, she tested the wind for prey and enemies.

She had not seen her sisters or brothers in many nights, nor had she come across their spoor. They had become vague memories of a different time and a different life. Now she was alone, and she liked it that way.

The valley was hers. She roamed it as she pleased, with occasional forays into the next valley to the west. Of late she had been roaming farther than ever, compelled by a strange urge.

On this particular night, her sensitive nose caught the scent of an animal she seldom encountered: a gopher. Gophers lived in burrows and rarely ventured to the surface. But the scent was strong, so she investigated, and was rewarded with the *scrtich* and *scratch* of its small claws. It was digging, and had its back to her.

The female knew how quickly gophers could disappear under the ground. Hunched low, she reached it in two bounds. A single swipe sufficed.

In a short while, temporarily fed and content, the female climbed toward the pass into the next valley. The wind whipped her, as it always did that high up, and brought with it another scent, one that brought her to a halt and caused all the hairs on her body to stand on end.

A strange eagerness came over her, an eagerness combined with a powerful hunger that was not a hunger at all, but something new.

She descended swiftly, too swiftly, and had to backtrack

a few times when she briefly lost the smell. Presently, she established that the source was a slope to the south. Unsure of her reception, she stalked silently forward. The *crunch* of a bone warned her she was close.

Over a rise lay a gully, and in the gully lay a large buck. Its neck had been ripped apart. Lying across it, greedily eating, was the buck's slayer.

The female hesitated. Part of her wanted to go nearer, part of her wanted to flee.

In a flash, the male was off the buck and crouched for combat. Growling ferociously, he advanced to attack, then jerked back as if surprised. He sniffed noisily, his head swinging from side to side.

The female waited. She was smaller, but it was he who came meekly forward and sniffed her where only a male dared sniff and only at times like this.

Later, the female made for the pass. She was hungry again, but she did not hunt. She wanted only to curl up in her den and sleep. Dimly, she sensed something special had taken place. She remembered her mother, and her siblings, and somehow—call it instinct, call it nature—she knew that one day not far off she would do as her mother had done and bring new life into the world. More of her kind to roam and hunt and kill.

The female would rear them as her mother had reared her. She would teach them the things they needed to know. And maybe, just maybe, she would take them down to the lake, to the log dens of the strange creatures with the long sticks that boomed like thunder, and they would feast on the strange creatures.

The female would like that. She would like that very much.

#48
WILDERNESS
LORD GRIZZLY
David Thompson

Nate King has a lot to be happy about. He and his family are settling into a new home, far from the taint of civilization. But the deep wilderness has its own set of dangers, including the greatest predator of them all: the giant grizzly. Nate has earned a reputation as Grizzly Killer, but this bear is different—this bear saved his life once, and Nate feels a debt of honor. But is it possible to teach a wild griz to go against its murderous nature? Will Nate's plan be any match for the mammoth bear's four-inch claws and wickedly sharp teeth? Or will his family learn a fatal lesson of their own?

EAST OF
THE BORDER
· JOHNNY D. BOGGS

Their names are legendary: Wild Bill Hickok, Buffalo
Bill Cody and Texas Jack Omohundro. The stories of
their infamous exploits are far more engrossing than any
dime novel. And now those stories would be shared with
the nation in a touring stage show called the Buffalo Bill
Combination. These great frontiersmen had no stage
experience, but they certainly could entertain. Acclaimed
author Johnny D. Boggs invites you behind the scenes to
hear what went on in the performers' own words, to see
for yourself the real men behind the tall tales.

LOUIS
L'AMOUR
A MAN CALLED TRENT

Louis L'Amour is one of the most popular, beloved and honored of all American authors. For many readers, his novels and stories have become the very definition of the Old West. Collected here are two of L'Amour's classic novellas, both featuring enigmatic gunfighter Lance Kilkenny. "The Rider of Lost Creek" was first published in a magazine as a novella, then, nearly thirty years later, expanded by L'Amour to novel length. This book presents, for the first time ever in paperback, the original version, as L'Amour first wrote it. "A Man Called Trent" was also written initially as a novella, only to be expanded many years later. Readers can once again enjoy it, restored to its original glory.

Dorchester Publishing Co., Inc.
P.O. Box 6640   __5600-3
Wayne, PA 19087-8640 $6.99 US/$8.99 CAN

Please add $2.50 for shipping and handling for the first book and $.75 for each additional book. NY and PA residents, add appropriate sales tax. No cash, stamps, or CODs. Canadian orders require $2.00 for shipping and handling and must be paid in U.S. dollars. Prices and availability subject to change. **Payment must accompany all orders.**

Name: _____

Address: _____

City: _____ State: _____ Zip: _____

E-mail: _____

I have enclosed $_____ in payment for the checked book(s).

CHECK OUT OUR WEBSITE! www.dorchesterpub.com
____ Please send me a free catalog.